PRAISE FOR PREVIOUS BOOKS

ARRESTED SONG

"Karafilly succeeds brilliantly where I had decided not to even try. A very accomplished novel."
—**Louis de Bernieres**

"*Arrested Song* is a wonderful novel, fully realized and absorbing."
—**Anna Porter**

"A gripping, powerfully evocative chronicle of Greek island life. Hard to put this book down."
—**Sofka Zinovieff**

"An epic, page-turning story of longing and bravery. *Arrested Song* is a must read."
—**Nadia Marks**

"One of the best novels I've read about modern Greece... A truly original work."
—**Diana Farr Louis**

THE HOUSE ON SELKIRK AVENUE

"A fascinating, subtle and very timely novel."
—**Stephen Vizinczey**

"*The House on Selkirk Avenue* evokes the political fervour and sizzling eroticism of Montreal during the War Measures Act. A rich, memorable read."
—**Anne Henderson**

"A terrific read!"
—**Jane Juska**

THE STRANGER IN THE PLUMED HAT

"A taut, expressive, and emotionally restrained exploration of a family's descent into Alzheimer's. I admired it greatly for its clarity and courage. Any family who has been to this dark place will derive comfort and instruction from her work."
—**Michael Ignatieff**

"An utterly moving, memorable, and haunting book – an extraordinary evocation of the relationship between a mother and a daughter, written with gentle h... with genuine passion, and with grace."
—**Jay Neugeboren**

"This is not only a richly human report of the devastation of Alzheimer's — hideous, poignant and ruefully funny; it is also an acknowledgement of how tangled and endlessly changing our memories of family turn out to be, long, long before the compromises of senility set in."
—**Rosellen Brown**

ASHES AND MIRACLES: A Polish Journey

"A brilliant, beautifully written, deeply moving book."
—**Josef Skvorecky**

"*Ashes and Miracles* is a sparkling and profound portrait of 1990s Poland, it is all here — the weariness, the hopes, the paradoxes, the layers of hatred and suffering, the unavoidable glare of history. Karafilly has a sharp eye and has used her considerable research with imagination."
—**Philip Marsden**

"Karafilly's Poland is a fascinating, unexpected place. She brings to her journey a passionate engagement, a keen eye, and a commitment to letting the people she meets come wonderfully alive."
—**Charles Foran**

"Part memoir, part history, part social commentary, *Ashes and Miracles* is a truly remarkable achievement."
—**Robert Weaver, CBC**

"Combining elements of both travelogue and autobiography, *Ashes and Miracles* seamlessly bridges the boundary between belles lettres and documentary. A subtle, sophisticated, and beautifully crafted book."
—**Elaine Kalman Naves**

NIGHT CRIES

"Karafilly seems to be present, psychologically, everywhere in that world. She becomes not only the tourist seeking a week of sun and cheap romance on the island, but the gnarled fisherman struggling to make a life there; not only the privileged, alienated outsider, but the restless, dissatisfied insider; not only the female, but the male. Her empathetic range is impressively broad. Karafilly's debut in this first book offers much pleasure, and makes one look forward eagerly to her next."
—**Roy MacSkimming**

TUNES FOR DANCING BEARS

OTHER BOOKS BY IRENA KARAFILLY

Arrested Song (2023)
The House on Selkirk Avenue (2017)
The Stranger in the Plumed Hat (2000)
Ashes and Miracles (1998)
Night Cries (1990)

Irena Karafilly

TUNES FOR DANCING BEARS

Baraka Books

Montréal

All rights reserved. No part of this book may be reproduced or transmitted in any form or by any means, electronic or mechanical, including photocopying, recording, or by any information storage and retrieval system, without permission in writing from the publisher.

© Irena Karafilly
www.irenakarafilly.com

ISBN 978-1-77186-381-0 pbk; 978-1-77186-389-6 epub;
978-1-77186-390-2 pdf

Cover by Leila Marshy
Book Design by Folio infographie
Editing: Leila Marshy
Proofreading: Anne Marie Marko

Legal Deposit, 2nd quarter 2025
Bibliothèque et Archives nationales du Québec
Library and Archives Canada

Published by Baraka Books of Montreal
Printed and bound in Quebec

TRADE DISTRIBUTION & RETURNS

Canada
UTP Distribution: UTPdistribution.com

United States
Independent Publishers Group: IPGbook.com

We acknowledge the support from the Société de développement des entreprises culturelles (SODEC) and the Government of Quebec tax credit for book publishing administered by SODEC.

For Diana Farr Louis

> "What would happen if one woman told the truth about her life? The world would split open."
>
> *Muriel Rukeyser*

MONDAY
September 2, 1991

1

The obstetrician seemed menacing. He looked like a shark: small eyes and stretched lips, and too many teeth when he opened his mouth to speak. He had given up trying to breathe life into her baby and was now leaning over her under the blinding lights. For a moment, nothing came out of his mouth but a puff of stale breath. And when at last he told her, muttering a word she did not understand, Lydia's own lips went stiff, as if numbed by novocaine. She became aware of silence, abrupt and furtive, and a sudden scuttling through the haze surrounding the birthing table.

A young nurse stopped by and, her mouth twitching, asked whether she wished to hold her baby. Lydia was still grappling for coherence. Only a short while earlier, gazing at herself in the overhead mirror, she'd had the feeling of participating in some sort of theatrical production: elaborate costumes and scenery, herself at centre stage, supine, obedient to the director, while a part of her struggled to wrest itself free of her possessive flesh.

She had been good, had been *wonderful*. They had all said so, urging her to push, push, push. And she wanted to go on being good; dreaded being abandoned in this vast, antiseptic chamber. At last, she accepted the stillborn child and held him stiffly in her arms, looking into his face with dream-like detachment. *Mine?* The room spun around. The child bore a remarkable resemblance to her husband.

But where was her husband? Someone had tried to call him after she'd been admitted, but John, a surgeon at another hospital, was on call during that long holiday weekend and not immediately reachable. She had forgotten all about him until just this moment.

Dr. Minnaar had left by then, closely followed by his assistants. Except for the young nurse, the room was empty, like a deserted theatre following a bomb threat. Had they forgotten her? Lydia felt paralyzed, overcome by a nightmarish terror of urgently needing to say something but finding her tongue frozen, her eloquent Greek hands dead. Her fingertips on the child's head registered no sensation.

"Your husband's on his way, Mrs. Gabriel," the nurse said. Gently. Then something else, something about the baby. *Anoxia.*

"What?"

Lydia's heart was a wild bird trapped inside a chimney. She held the inert child for another moment then thrust him back at the young nurse, who looked doomed, having failed to escape along with her colleagues.

"Do something!" Lydia heard herself shout, her body shuddering as though subjected to electric shock. "Do something, please!"

"You're still young, Mrs. Gabriel. You—"

She was thirty-three going on thirty-four but did not argue. All she said was "No!" The word reverberated in the empty room while her head rolled on the pillow. "No!" Nothing else, just the one word uttered over and over, like an amplifier of her shrivelling heart. "No!"

A few minutes passed. Another nurse came in, checked her pulse, took her blood pressure. Then, murmuring words of comfort, she administered a sedative.

All this took place in early September, that short fickle period between seasons. By the time her husband arrived, Lydia Gabriel had been moved out of the birthing area and onto the bustling maternity ward, where she slept for several merciful hours. Every now and then, though, she muttered in her sleep, speaking in her mother tongue.

"Panagía mou! Panagía, voíthisé me!"

2

By mid-afternoon, John had been with his wife for three hours, going out now and then for a cup of coffee. He'd been out when Lydia asked to see her son again. Though he was aware that hospitals were now encouraging parents to spend time with a stillborn infant, he had doubts about this particular practice.

He stood there, arms at his sides, and watched in grim silence as his wife communed with their lifeless child. She held him gingerly at first, then quickly began to roll back the blanket, her lips quivering as a tiny white hand emerged from within the blue wool.

Nauseated, John turned toward the nurse, a large, brassy-haired Englishwoman called Mrs. Atkinson. He did not like her. She stood by the door with the respectful, slightly obsequious air of an undertaker. He supposed she had been instructed to stay there but held it against her all the same. He knew her type: conscientious, dull. Couldn't she leave them for a moment—go fill the jug with water, clear the untouched lunch tray? He looked at her coldly, relishing his aversion.

And yet, only that morning, Mrs. Atkinson had seemed to him both thoughtful and efficient. He had been glad for Lydia who, he knew from past experience, liked chatty nurses. Mrs. Atkinson spared herself no trouble, rubbing Lydia's legs (they had at one point begun to shake violently), murmuring in her ear. She had even noticed *his* hand, which he had injured in his rush to get to St. Margaret's, and offered to have it bandaged while a young resident went about examining his wife. Though John had declined, embarrassed, he had been grateful for the nurse's kindness.

"I'll be back in a few minutes," she said now. "Buzz if you need anything." Smiling shakily, she turned and bustled out, leaving them alone with their dead child between them. The room smelled faintly of disinfectant or floor cleaner. John felt a sudden urge to flee.

Having on occasion been witness to his Greek relatives' emotional outbursts, he had expected his wife to shriek and howl the moment she saw the child. Instead, she seemed to him to go quietly insane, acting as if the baby were still alive! She had unwrapped the blanket and, perhaps surprised to find the child stark naked, gave the slightly raised window an anxious glance, as if worried the child might catch a cold.

"He's beautiful, isn't he?" she said in a small voice, as if speaking to herself.

John both heard and didn't hear her. "If only I had come in time," he said, raking his hand through his hair. "Of course, it's ridiculous. What could I have done? Still, I do feel I should have been there."

He had been performing emergency gallbladder surgery when they tried to reach him, but rushed to St. Margaret's the moment he got the message. It was too late. Lydia had been alone during the delivery. Ironically—unluckily—it was Labour Day and he had been on call at the Jewish General. He could only imagine how his wife must have felt at the dreadful moment when she registered the newborn's silence. She still seemed unable to process the tragedy, tenderly stroking the baby's abundant black hair: like mine, John caught himself thinking. *Mine.*

"It's not your fault," Lydia said in a toneless voice. "Stop blaming yourself." She had taken so long to answer he forgot that he had spoken. "Emmanuel," she whispered, her hand caressing the baby's head, lingering on cheeks, white and still as wax, on tiny, translucent earlobes.

The child seemed to be sleeping. He looked, to John, far from beautiful. His ears were too large, his head like a melon squashed by a careless shopper. But all this was normal. He felt awed and oddly relieved. Lydia was fondling the hardening body: the tiny toes, the penis.

John shifted his gaze toward the window. It was a grey afternoon, with faint, intermittent sunshine. The need to flee made him want to throw up. The room was suddenly stuffy, faintly redolent of the covered lunch: meatloaf and overcooked broccoli. He had not eaten all day and was not tempted to now, hating hospital food even at the best of times. Still, the nausea might be partly due to hunger.

He closed his eyes and drew in a steadying breath. The moment passed. Music—something achingly beautiful—was playing in a nearby room.

"Dr. Laplante, Dr. Misra, Dr. Paul Harris."

The P.A. system repeated the doctors' names over and over, loud and urgent. It occurred to John that he might not be able to operate for some time. His hand was beginning to swell.

A few silent minutes went by.

"He has your mouth, doesn't he?" he said at length. It was the only kind thought that came to him just then. Lydia had striking amber-hued eyes and beautiful, sculpted lips.

"Oh, you really think so?" Absurdly, his lame words could still offer pleasure. John observed this with a spasm of guilt. But that, too, passed, giving way to a small apprehension. Hearing the clatter of trays out in the hall, he worried that someone—a nurse or a kitchen aide—might suddenly poke her head in and bring an end to their private communion.

No one came; no one even knocked. Was Mrs. Atkinson standing guard? he wondered. Though he had taken off his jacket, the room seemed increasingly stifling. He became aware of a creeping sense of loss, an emptiness on the edge of tears that put him in mind of a long-ago operation which, despite his best efforts, failed to save the patient.

"Lydia?" A sudden chill descended on him. His wife was turning the child this way and that, peering between buttocks, thumbing the spine, the skull. Her hair, which had gone prematurely white in her twenties, was a jumble of curls. Her hospital gown had come loose at the top.

"Darling," he said. "May I...hold him for a moment?" It was like tugging on a painful molar. Only the tooth in this case had ached for a brief, intense spell, then inexplicably stopped.

"Oh! Do you want to? I didn't think you would," she said, much too loudly. "I'm sorry," she murmured.

He bent down and reached for the baby, quickly, awkwardly, overcome by a brief, dizzying spell. He had irritated his hand, picking up the child, and now held it out, throbbing, like a mendicant.

Lydia was staring at him. "What happened to your hand?"

"Oh, nothing. Nothing serious. I jammed it in my car door." Though he had spoken matter-of-factly, John's senses had all at once gone awry. The injured hand, the stiff body in his arms, a sudden dryness in his mouth—he experienced all these through a sort of haze.

"Trying to hurry over?"

"Yes." He shrugged dismissively. "It's nothing." Ashamed of his own clumsiness, he felt once more the threat of suppressed tears. His arms felt strained, his pulse uncomfortably rapid. The baby seemed exceptionally long for a newborn, and very slender. Clearly, his own frame. "He's really big, isn't he?"

"A little over eight pounds." Lydia's mouth quivered. "Where was all that weight, I wonder. I wasn't very big, was I?"

"No. I don't think so." John's heart stirred, casting loose the memory of Lydia coming home from the gynaecologist's office, telling him she was finally pregnant. They had by then been married for eleven years. There had been an abortion early in their relationship, and then a miscarriage not long after their honeymoon. "You were normal, I guess."

He sat down, thinking: My third child. There had been a time when he longed to have a child. His parents, too, had fervently hoped for a grandson. By the time Lydia had conceived for the third time, though, John was dismayed to find himself feeling occasional doubts.

"I really watched my diet this time," Lydia was saying, speaking in the same toneless voice. She'd kept some sort of diet last time too, John vaguely recalled. But later, when she miscarried in her fourth month, her appetite became voracious. It was then that she began growing somewhat fleshy, and quickly, astoundingly, white-haired.

John's mind dwelled on all this rather chaotically. He was wondering whether he'd held the child long enough. His stomach began to rumble.

"There's no flaw on him anywhere," Lydia said. "I've looked twice now." She had reverted to Greek, which she did now and then, in highly stressed moments.

John kept his thoughts to himself. He stood up and was about to hand the child back to his wife when Mrs. Atkinson returned, flushed and breathless, trailing a faint, medicinal smell.

"I'm so sorry, things are a little hectic today." She trotted toward Lydia and, blinking like a startled owl, reached for the baby.

"No. Not yet, please." Lydia levered herself up on an elbow. "Is it all right if I snip off a bit of his hair?"

"Why not? He's your baby." Mrs. Atkinson achieved a smile. She pulled a pair of scissors from one of her side pockets. "He looks an awful lot like his Daddy, doesn't he?"

"You think so?" Lydia—both women—turned their eyes toward John. He was standing near the foot of the bed, motionless but for his working jaw. *Daddy.*

Mrs. Atkinson made a soft, clucking sound. "You should have let me bandage that hand, Dr. Gabriel." She bent down to assist Lydia. "Would you like me to get someone to do it for you?"

"No. Thank you though."

John felt a stab of self-pity and was instantly swept by a wave of shame. He watched helplessly as Mrs. Atkinson supported the child's dark head while Lydia clutched the scissors: *snip snip*, on one side. And again, *snip, snip*, on the other. He had, until that moment, thought it only figurative when someone expressed the need to pinch himself. He felt it was surely a dream, a scene out of some surreal film. Out on the street, an ambulance siren wailed but did not quite drown out what the nurse was saying.

"We could have a picture taken for you—if you'd like, my dear."

"Yes! Oh yes," Lydia said. "Why didn't *I* think of that?"

"I'm going down for coffee," John heard himself say. "You probably want some time alone with... him."

"Yes." Lydia didn't look up. "You must have something to eat, John," she added mechanically.

"I might. I am feeling a little queasy." He stood rubbing his jaw. "I think I'll get my hand bandaged while I am downstairs," he said, shivering with a desperate need to get away—not only from his wife and lifeless child but from the noise and bustle of this entire maternity ward.

"Oh, Dr. Gabriel." He had just reached the threshold when Mrs. Atkinson's voice stopped him. I am not going back, he thought, even as he half-turned.

"Yes?"

"Would you mind stopping at the station on your way back?" She smiled, the scissors glinting in her hand. "There's some forms which—"

"Yes, yes, of course," he said, perhaps a little too quickly. He was about to close the door behind him when an infant began to squall somewhere down the hall. He took a deep breath, inwardly cursing the shrill newborn whose howling drowned out everything around him. Where was the child's mother? Where were the fucking nurses?

He felt a brief, unfocused rage shake him, fading only when a young nursing student came breezing down from the main nursing station. Dressed in a crisp, blue-striped uniform, the redhead rolled her eyes dramatically and flashed him a quirky, complicitous smile, presumably reserved for all new fathers. When John blinked helplessly, the girl mouthed something he failed to make out; just a few quick words that, for unfathomable reasons, made him recoil inwardly, then stagger across the corridor toward the opening elevator.

3

When she first suspected that she might be pregnant, Lydia told no one, not even her husband. She bought a test kit at the neighbourhood pharmacy and that Saturday, alone at home, unwrapped it with shaky fingers.

She waited, darting in and out of the bathroom for a chaotic, interminable spell, until, at last, the tiny mirror under the glass tube showed a bright orange ball, like a small blazing sun. Outside, a blizzard was raging. Inside, bed and lamps and dresser spun until she reached the phone, where she paused for a moment, hesitated, then called her mother, who was not home; then her husband, who was operating; then her sister-in-law, Helen, who had become her closest friend and who, fortunately, happened to be in town.

Lydia's brother and his family were away on their annual Greek vacation, but, waiting for Helen, Lydia managed to squeeze in a call to Marika Lehotay, another close friend, as well as to her younger sister, who was studying in Toronto. Cars honked their horns. The front lawn blurred with dancing snowflakes. She wanted to fling the windows open and holler at the cars below, "I am pregnant!" The neighbour's door was slammed after a UPS delivery and she mouthed to the messenger's departing back: "I'm pregnant!" A bird landed on a snow-wrapped branch and she brought her face close to the glass and whispered to it: "I'm pregnant." She said it to her own reflection in the bathroom mirror, and then to a black-and-white photo of her late father as a young Greek soldier on his first furlough.

She kept trying her parents' phone and finally, just before Helen rang the bell an hour later, her mother returned home from the market. Lydia blurted the news which, in Greek, made her stammer for some reason, as if she were saying now what she had not dared say when she'd found herself pregnant at twenty, or even the second time, at twenty-two, about to get married. She did not understand the clenching in her stomach, until her mother, momentarily shrill with joy, snapped in Greek, "Don't tell anyone yet!" Then, with sobriety, "You must be very careful this time, Lydia."

Her mother said this so often throughout her pregnancy that, in time, Lydia stopped answering; quit trying to reason when urged to wear an evil-eye charm; walked away when nagged to stop working, eat daily fish soup, nap in the afternoon. The doctor assured her *this* pregnancy was perfectly normal.

There was no spotting this time, no need whatsoever for excessive caution. Lydia believed him because she not only felt better than she had the last time but stronger than she had in years. She was drowsy sometimes and occasionally nauseated but she never again threw up and her appetite became legendary.

She remained active, rolling her eyes when her mother's Greek friends warned her against driving a car, walking past strangers' dogs, venturing out in storms. A dog's snarl, a sudden clap of thunder—a single moment of fright and the child she carried might be in sudden danger, they said.

How she laughed at them all, village crones who wagged their heads when she told them, smiling, you could no more shake loose a good egg than an unripe apple from an apple tree. It was what Dr. Minnaar had told her—the gynaecologist, she reminded them—but the women only sucked their teeth and sighed. A doctor was a doctor but they knew what they knew. You couldn't learn in medical school all there was to life, could you? No, she should be more careful. Did the doctor tell her how important it was, how absolutely crucial, to satisfy a pregnant woman's cravings? He didn't?

"Well, there you are!" said her mother, speaking in the dialect of her birthplace, a coastal village on the Aegean island of Lesbos. "Doctors don't know everything about a woman's needs, do they?"

All this came back to taunt Lydia as she lay watching Mrs. Atkinson whisk away her baby. *Emmanuel.* An odd feeling took over her body; an abrupt sensation of emptiness, as if she had been drained of blood, and a violent desire for replenishment that seemed larger somehow than her longing for the child himself. She did not, in any case, believe that it was irrevocable, though her flesh felt hollowed out and her mind intent on its frenzied scrutiny of the recent past.

There had been times. Times when she hadn't been sure that John really wanted a child. He surprised her, asking to hold the baby just now. She felt oddly detached from her former self—as if she were watching a vaguely familiar stranger, or fragments from the nightmares she'd had while she carried Emmanuel.

For, despite an apparently normal pregnancy, she had suffered those from time to time; had seen herself giving birth to the Elephant Man, to a Down Syndrome baby, to twins suffering from spina bifida. It was at night that these fears assailed her and she never spoke of them—not to anyone. She felt as if mere verbalization had the power to actuate her nightmares; not only words but worries.

Having read that a mother's state of mind was transmittable through the placenta to her child, Lydia spent her days rallying happy thoughts. When her husband worked late, as he did at least once a week, she read a dozen books on childcare, as well as picture books, Scandinavian fairy tales, parents' magazines.

One day, cleaning out the attic, she read in an old issue of *TIME* how, upon being told that her son would be executed, Gary Gilmore's mother had reportedly said: "I knew from the day he was born he would come to no good, that one."

The quote had brought on a small internal tumult. Had she been able to, Lydia would have rushed to the phone to demand, "How, how?" What could a newborn do, after all, that would hint at the future of a murderer? And even allowing for postpartum blues, how could a new mother have such vile thoughts about her own child?

Unable to answer her own questions, Lydia found herself wondering what Hitler's mother might have thought, cradling her newborn son. How did the infant Stalin seem to his mother? Einstein? Michelangelo?

She remembered her own mother, who was at home with a retired nurse, recovering from a varicose-vein operation and looking forward to the birth of another grandchild. The thought sent an arrow of pain through her clogged chest.

Oh my God, how will I tell my mother?

4

Sometime in January, when Lydia was in the first trimester of her pregnancy, Dr. John Gabriel went for a late lunch in the Jewish General Hospital's coffee shop and, waiting for his grilled cheese sandwich, saw Claire Remington come in.

A colleague's ex-wife, Claire was a marriage counsellor affiliated with the hospital: a tall, dark-haired Brit with a Cleopatra haircut and hooded, sage-green eyes that somehow seemed omniscient. John, regarded by his own Greek family as an Englishman *manqué*, had always thought Claire the most attractive of the surgeons' wives; he had even once, at a Christmas party, drunk too much and flirted with her a little.

He was not the only admirer. There had been rumours of infidelities on both sides and, three years back, even more tantalizing gossip following a New Year's Eve party at a ski chalet. In Montreal's staid circles of physicians and surgeons, the Remingtons—Kenneth with his BMW motorbike and Claire with her published poems and solitary trips to remote destinations like Nepal or Bali—were generally regarded as somewhat bohemian. When their marriage broke up last year, there was no end to the speculation and departmental jokes—inevitable perhaps, given Claire's occupation; understandable, given colleagues' lust and envy.

For here was a woman, alone at the challenging age of forty but showing no sign whatsoever of inner anxiety. It was understood that the Remingtons' had been an amicable divorce (they were seen having lunch together on at least two occasions), though in time Claire would tell John that a goodwill divorce was like having all one's teeth extracted and still having to smile.

But this was as far as Claire would ever come—with John at any rate—in alluding to post-marital woes. With her only daughter at the Ontario College of Art (where, coincidentally, Lydia's sister was studying graphic design), Claire wasted no time setting herself up in a chic Old Montreal condo and opting for a four-day work week in order to do something she had always longed to do: try her hand at writing a mystery novel with a hospital setting.

All this, and much else besides, Claire had told John during that first coffee-shop lunch. They seemed, in the space of an hour, to have covered everything from insomnia—an affliction they shared—to psychoanalysis, which Claire had, in her youth, considered taking up as a profession, and which still held a certain attraction for her. It was, she joked, the only profession that might have made it possible for her to sleep on the job and wake up to talk about others' dreams.

John was dazzled and made no secret of it. It amused him to think that both his wife and his mistress seemed to have literary interests, which held little appeal for him.

They agreed to have lunch again, a proper one this time, at a fine Italian restaurant called QUAI SERA. Claire had been the one to suggest the place. They drank their first bottle of wine chuckling over the establishment's name.

The lunch was the first of several, leading in due course to an elegant dinner at Claire's condo, and eventually, to John's first and only extramarital affair. He knew that he was not as worldly as Claire. He also knew, because she'd told him so, that she was enjoying their strong sexual rapport.

What distinguished Claire from most women was her lack of sentimentality. Although he sometimes accused her of being an incorrigible cynic, he found her independence and ironic mindset oddly exhilarating. Even the most routine of her observations often carried an epigrammatic weight. Occasionally, she reminded him of his sister, Helen, who was a journalist, and who kept a notebook at her bedside, jotting down quotations from the books she read, dropping *bon mots* into her conversations the way others might drop the names of fine wines or celebrity acquaintances.

What surprised John was the quality of Claire's attention: her listening skills, her deep reserves of patience and sympathy. Whether through professional training or personal interest, she gradually made it possible for him to open up in wholly unexpected ways. He had never, even in the early, most troubled days of his marriage, considered seeking professional help. Yet here he was now, on the threshold to middle age, sharing his private life with a glamorous woman who was a professional marriage counsellor and also, incredible as it seemed, his secret mistress! His one guilty secret.

And he did feel guilty, even after it occurred to him that Claire's chief attraction actually lay in her perspicacity. He could not imagine anyone more deserving of her name. The sexual pull was undeniable, but great sex was something many other women might have offered and, until pregnancy changed everything, even his own wife had. He'd had no complaints on that score before that. None whatsoever.

John was aware that, both professionally and socially, he had a reputation for being reserved, so he was all the more astonished by his sudden capacity for self-revelation. Though there were still some things he could not quite bring himself to voice, he had never confided in anyone to quite this extent. That Claire could be both his lover and an apparently dispassionate listener seemed to him like nothing short of a gift, though one frequently chafing at his conscience: he had always thought of himself as an honourable man.

But even this problem he was eventually able to air with the woman he had teasingly taken to calling Dr. Claire. He had grown so accustomed to unburdening himself to her that his first thought on finally escaping St. Margaret's maternity ward had been: I must go and see Claire. As soon as possible!

He could not, unfortunately, do so today. After leaving the ward, he felt duty-bound to visit both Lydia's mother and his own parents. Approaching his family's home, he experienced an overwhelming sense of loss and, at the same time, an irrational spurt of shame, like a promising schoolboy forced to face his family with an unexpectedly disappointing report card.

His fiercely ambitious mother had disapproved of his marriage to a poor stonemason's daughter, unaware that Lydia was already pregnant. Although he always made it a point to defend his wife and his mother to each other, John thought that Lydia was more often than not in the right. His aging mother, who had once been beautiful and lively, was turning into a moody drama queen.

There was no doubting her genuine distress on hearing about the stillbirth. All the same, because he knew her well, John could not help noting the involuntary narrowing of her eyes, a tell-tale tightening of the lips. All her doubts about her son's marriage had finally been validated. He could see his mother thinking this as plainly as if the bitter words had actually been uttered.

And yet, when he told her just before leaving that Lydia did not wish to have visitors for now, his mother wrapped herself in a wounded, faintly martyred air, as if she had extended a helping hand, only to find it rudely and inexplicably slapped away.

And then there was Lydia's mother. Poor Antigone behaved exactly as he might have expected. She pulled at her grey hair and all but banged her head against her living room wall.

"Holy Virgin, dear Christ, this will kill her...she'll die of heartbreak, my child!"

She went on keening in this manner—on and on and on. John escaped as soon as he decently could, his own heart weeping for his devastated wife, all alone with her grief in a cold hospital room. He promised his mother-in-law to keep in touch, gave her a quick hug, then left. It was close to midnight by the time he arrived home, aching from head to toe.

It had been one of the worst days of his life and it was hard to see how the rest of the week might offer anything by way of relief. He longed for oblivion, dreading the thought of morning as a death-row inmate might dread the dawn of his execution. He took two Tylenols, drank a glass of milk, and went straight to bed. It was too late to be making phone calls.

TUESDAY
September 3, 1991

5

"Help! Help!"

Lydia awoke with an odd kicking sensation in her womb. Slowly, she rolled her head toward the moonlit window, groping for clarity. It was still dark outside; strong winds were flapping at the windowpanes. She was in an unfamiliar room, her right arm painfully lodged under her head. For some reason, she was unable to free it, feeling herself totter on the edge of a dream, while the gusting wind slapped at her muddled consciousness.

It was not until her eyes fell on the ID bracelet circling her wrist that full awareness struck. There was a moment of icy pain, through which, dimly, Lydia began to feel a struggling perplexity. Her cries for help had burst out of a tortured dream, but she was no longer dreaming. She knew that for certain—or would have had it not been for the persistent kicking in her womb; a deeply familiar sensation that, right now, made no sense whatsoever.

Am I going mad?

She forced herself to review yesterday's events—the rushed delivery, the first moment of slashing comprehension. *Stillborn.*

And yet, though she was now fully awake and lucid, the kicking in her womb remained as indisputable as the weather.

For some reason, both her arms ached, as if, hypnotized, she had carried some immense burden only her muscles had a memory of. She found the other pain, the one between her legs, almost reassuring, for she remembered its origin well enough; recalled the OBS resident's balding head, bent over his patchwork like a weary tailor.

It was the kicking that finally made Lydia reach for the bedside phone; the kicking and the lurking fear that she might indeed be going mad. She had an aunt who had been briefly institutionalized back in Greece, and a father whose behaviour had always been a little erratic.

Just then, the evening nurse stepped in and Lydia put down the phone, gasping in pain as she rolled over to face a diminutive young woman named Charmaine Syn.

A moment passed, during which the nurse's eyelids fluttered, looking almost flirtatious. Lydia became acutely aware of her own odious body: swollen and slashed and malodourous, oozing blood and sweat. She wished she could summon the strength to fling open the door and holler into the hectic corridor:

My baby has died! He died and they won't even tell me why!

No, she would not tell them about the kicking—would not confide in any of them—though the sensation in her womb showed no sign of abating.

There was also the discomfort of a full bladder. She hoped it would not have to be relieved again with the help of a catheter. Yet why should she care about any of that now? How—having been poked and pawed and slashed and patched up, having been left hollow—how could she still care about the failure to void of her own accord?

"Your urethra is bruised, that's all," the nurse said. "Please do not worry."

She patted Lydia's shoulder, gave her a quick injection, then left the room, her white shoes squeaking. Rain was falling, sifting down from a low, bruised-looking sky. The kicking in Lydia's womb gradually stopped and, after a while, she found herself staring fixedly at a shaft of dust motes before drifting off again toward more tranquil shores.

6

Sometime before dawn, John Gabriel leapt up from a bad dream, hair on end, pyjamas drenched in sweat. In his dream, he was operating on a patient who needed a simple laparoscopy. For some reason, John had decided on the more invasive laparotomy and the anaesthetized patient woke up screaming, leapt off the operating table, and dropped dead on the floor.

John had no idea what had brought on this dream, but he went on cowering in its shadows, his heart thudding under the light duvet, every bone in his body pleading for sleep.

But sleep eluded him in those murky hours. His mouth tasted foul. His head was throbbing. He thought the heavy perspiration might be due to fever, but when he reached into the bedside drawer for the thermometer, it was missing.

A weary sigh escaped his chest. Lydia had more than her share of domestic skills, but keeping things in their proper place was not one of them. The thermometer might be in one of two medicine cabinets, or in a kitchen cupboard, or, for all he knew, even in the downstairs solarium. He was not about to go looking for it, if only because he knew that failure to find it was likely to raise not only his temperature but also his blood pressure.

To make matters worse, his nose was stuffy and his throat scratchy. Fumbling in another drawer, he found some honey lozenges left over from his last bout with the flu. He popped one in his mouth, then trudged to the bathroom to relieve himself, carefully avoiding his own reflection while he washed his hands and gargled with mouthwash. He returned to bed, still hoping against hope that the gods might take pity on him.

The gods seeming wholly indifferent, John sat up and reached for his reading glasses with a heavy sigh.

On his bedside table, there was a biography of Flaubert that Lydia had tried to foist on him. Biographies often put him to sleep but, alas, not tonight. Tonight, he could neither sleep nor focus on the minutiae of Gustave Flaubert's life. He kept turning pages without registering content, coughing from time to time, dabbing at his stuffy nose.

On Lydia's side of the bed, he suddenly remembered, there was a tiny jar of eucalyptus ointment she liked to use whenever she had a cold. Rubbing his eyes, he eased himself across the king-sized bed and pulled out Lydia's drawer, his eyes falling on her leather-bound journal. Vaguely, he had always known the journal was there; Lydia had never been in the least secretive about it, possibly because she knew he had no interest in her private musings.

On this particular night, though, still courting sleep, John found himself vaguely curious about Lydia's scribbling. She was, he knew, a worrywart by nature, but no doubt because he was, more often than not, inclined to be dismissive, she had usually kept her worries to herself. During her pregnancy, though, she could not suppress what often seemed to him like overblown anxieties. It occurred to him that, not having his ear, she may have been confiding her thoughts in her journal. Did she complain about him, his unwillingness to take her fears seriously? Would she be lying in her hospital bed now, feeling her fears had been vindicated?

All this was going through John's head when, only a little hesitant, he opened the stiff covers of his wife's journal and started to skim some of the recent entries. He did not expect to find marital secrets, but it came to him suddenly that if *he* had a guilty secret, it was not inconceivable that Lydia did as well.

At this point, John's conscience sent him an admonitory message and he hastened to put the journal back in its place. He had, however, read enough to be impressed by his wife's writing.

This should not have come as a surprise—Lydia had graduated from McGill at the top of her English class. If he was surprised, it was only because, unlike him and his sister, who were born in Montreal, she had come to Canada at the age of twelve and spoke Greek to her own family. Yet her writing, he reluctantly noted, was much better than his own. He had no gift for languages, so Lydia's facility with words seemed to him all the more remarkable. She worked for a small literary press, so he knew she had long since mastered English grammar and spelling. What surprised him was her ability to turn trivial domestic incidents into a compelling narrative.

The truth was: his wife often surprised him. She had, when he married her, seemed wholesome, unaffected, uncomplicated, yet eleven years of marriage had gradually revealed inevitable contradictions. He had observed, for example, that while Lydia professed to be an atheist, she also seemed to believe that some things were divinely preordained. She had her simpler moments. She could be as down to earth as a peasant and, despite fervent denials, occasionally superstitious. Yet she was both academically and artistically gifted. She took marvelous photographs whenever they travelled and liked to speculate on the lives of strangers, imagining what might have happened: if only this had taken place, if only that hadn't. Hers was a mind intent on giving everything shape and meaning.

One day he'd overheard her with one of her young nephews, telling him a bedtime story she'd made up on the spot.

"I think you just might be what they call a natural storyteller," he told her later that night. They were in their own bedroom by then, both of them reading.

"You think so?" She stopped and smiled at him.

"I do. Why don't you take a creative writing course?" he asked. He couldn't help but think of Claire, who had at some point taken such courses at Concordia University. Lydia was smart and imaginative but had to be pushed. She always had to be pushed, but then ended up exceeding everyone's expectations.

"Oh, I don't know." She stopped to ponder it for a long moment. "Well, okay, maybe I will. Why not?"

The impulse to concoct stories, she eventually told her husband, was something she must have inherited from her wildly imaginative father. She found storytelling as compelling as he once seemed to, sitting on the beach or in their own garden, regaling his children with stories from Greek mythology, or his own febrile imagination.

But if his wife was more complicated than he had initially suspected, John had become something of an enigma to himself. There was no question that he had become deeply attached to his wife, yet how to explain the fact that, early on, when his attachment had still been rather tenuous, it had never crossed his mind to be unfaithful to Lydia, whereas now, a decade or so into their marriage, he had allowed himself to slip into an extramarital affair?

At this, a deeper sigh escaped John. He had at some point decided that he must bring an end to his relationship with Claire before Lydia, or one of his colleagues, caught wind of it. He had resolved to do so as soon as his son was born, never expecting to find himself faced with a birth tragedy.

And it did still feel like a tragedy to him, despite the fact that he'd not been without worries about the inevitable demands of family life. Although he had barely acknowledged this even to himself, he had feared that, like most people, he and Lydia would quickly slide into a hectic existence revolving around childcare, chauffeuring, endless shopping for toys and clothes, visits to doctors, playgrounds. Did he, at this late stage, have what it took to be a fully committed father?

John glanced at the clock again, then at the glimmering window. Finally, with a long exhalation, he gave up any hope of getting back to sleep. Turning the alarm off, he swung his feet to the floor, then sat on the edge of the bed for a while before somehow summoning the strength to shave and take a long shower.

Having accomplished this, he limped downstairs to the kitchen, assaulted by worries about Lydia's emotional state. He had always been quick to find escape in his work or his history books (his mother had, early in his childhood, liked to call him a "book-eater" in Greek, and later on, an ostrich).

There was no escape now. His sister, to whom he was close, was away and did not even know about the stillbirth. After nine months of tense waiting, he had neither baby nor professional challenges to keep his mind from straying in hopeless directions. All he had was a grieving wife, devastated parents, and a secret, rather aloof, mistress.

The word *mistress* brought on a ripple of fresh guilt, though sex was the farthest thing from his mind these days. What he desperately needed was someone astute and smart in whom he could confide without fear of being judged. Had his sister been in town, he might have sought comfort in her company. But Helen was in Mexico, interviewing for some new CBC program. He knew she was due back sometime in early September, but when, exactly?

John sighed, his musings interrupted by their two cats, who were weaving between his feet, shrilly demanding their breakfast. He hastened to feed them, then stared out the bleak window, waiting for toast and coffee.

It promised to be a mild but gusty day. The windows were still dark, but he could hear the wind sporting with the branches on their old maple tree. Autumn was now just around the corner. Soon, their front lawn would be blanketed by dying leaves, blowing hither and thither, waiting for snow. Would his wife have the wherewithal to endure the long, icy winter that lay ahead?

7

A man was standing at the foot of her bed: a tall man with wiry hair and light brown eyes as melancholy as a basset hound's. He wore a white coat and was studying a chart when Lydia's eyes flew open.

A new doctor.

It was going on 8 a.m. Through the wall came a baby's muffled cry. Lydia's lips tasted salty. When she pulled the white sheet up to her chin, the stranger raised his gaze.

"Hello." He wore a vaguely apologetic smile. "I'm Dr. Seager, Dr. Minnaar's associate." The infant went on crying. "I'm very sorry. Dr. Minnaar—"

"I...I know." Lydia tried to sit up, breaking in on his explanation. "He told me before he left." Had said, that last time in his office, she would have to hurry if she wanted him to have the honour. She had been nine days overdue; he was scheduled to leave for South Africa.

"I'm very sorry," Dr. Seager repeated. He put the chart aside. "I know how hard it must be, having to deal with a stranger at a time like this."

"Yes...thank you." Lydia closed her eyes. The baby had stopped crying and, in the sudden silence, the wind could be heard, flapping and moaning.

"How do you feel?" the doctor asked. "I don't mean to sound obtuse but...I hoped you might tell me, if...if you can bring yourself to talk to me." He sat down beside her, holding on to the stethoscope but looking calm and patient, as if he had dropped in for nothing more than a friendly chat. "You must be angry," he stated when she did not answer.

"Yes." She was nervously fidgeting with her wedding ring.

"Well," he said, "you've got every right to feel cheated: nine months of waiting wiped out in one day."

"Yes." She stirred, looking at him more closely. "I don't suppose you know anything...?" She fell abruptly silent. The smell of smoke—real or imaginary, she really couldn't tell—was rising in her nostrils.

He shook his head in mute sympathy. "No, but—"

Afraid she might lose her nerve, she quickly cut in. "There seems to be something wrong with me." She spoke in an odd, mumbling voice, her heart wild.

"Oh? Would you like to tell me about it?" His gaze held her patiently, weary and sorrowful.

"I think I'm going mad." She'd let the word slip out, then raised her hands and hid her face behind them. The wind rose and fell, whistling at the windows. She said, "I keep feeling the baby kicking."

"Well...it does sound kind of crazy, doesn't it?" He sighed, raking his hand through his unruly hair. "Actually, though, it's not at all unusual." His eyes implored her to trust him. "Have you ever heard of phantom legs with amputees?" he asked.

"I guess so."

"It's the same sort of thing. Nothing to worry about, believe me," he added. "Anything else you think I should know?"

"I don't know...yes...my arms felt strange earlier—I can't quite describe it. Also, I keep...smelling smoke."

He looked at her for a moment. "Listen. Whatever you do, don't be afraid to talk about it; it's all...perfectly normal, trust me."

Normal then to feel that some part of you, some indispensable organ like your heart or your liver, was suddenly extracted from your body. Bitterly, she said, "I guess it's also normal, even banal, to say that I want to die but...I really do. I—" Her voice cracked.

"Mrs. Gabriel—Lydia—" He touched her arm lightly. "Look, I don't want to sound pompous but there are times, you know, when it takes more courage to live than to die." His glance fell on the empty tissue box next to her breakfast tray. He offered his own pack. "Please believe me, you'll get over this. In time," he added.

"Thank you." Though she wore nothing but a hospital gown, Lydia was perspiring profusely. "The thing is I can't...I just can't imagine picking up where I left off—can't imagine even going home." *Home.* A tiny sound, like a child's hiccup, escaped her throat. Her eyelids trembled as she turned to face him. "When am I being discharged?"

"Well." He stood up decisively, a dent between his eyebrows. "I'll have to examine you." The apologetic note was back in his voice.

"Right now?"

He smiled at her sadly, pulling out a pair of rubber gloves. "I'll try to be gentle."

"Okay." She was swept with gratitude for his patience, his exceptional kindness. Dr. Minnaar had been so hasty, so arrogant! "I'm sorry," she muttered vaguely. Her legs had begun to shake again. She fought the urge to flee, to hide the empty mountain of flesh rising beneath her breasts.

But soon this moment, too, passed. She felt herself grow resigned under his searching hands. Somewhere in the distance, a dog was barking; clouds drifted across the autumnal sky. She lay back, she rolled over, she followed his commands.

What if I hadn't gone into labour yesterday; waited until Minnaar had left and this gentler doctor took over—would everything still be the same?

She quivered under the stethoscope, his gloved fingers palpating her flesh. The tone of her bladder was impaired, Dr. Seager explained; her urethra was swollen.

"Why?"

He sighed and folded his stethoscope. "Big baby, quick delivery—not unusual."

He spoke soothingly. She would have to stay, though, until the problem cleared up. "I'll put you on medication...hopefully by tomorrow—"

She bowed her head, echoing bleakly. "Tomorrow."

"Yes...you mustn't give up on the future," he said. "One day at a time," he added, giving each word its own beat.

8

It was too early to call Claire. John finished his breakfast, washed a few dishes, then phoned the OR to confirm the week's cancelled surgeries. He thought of calling Lydia but she, too, would probably be asleep. He went back to the bedroom, put on a fresh pullover and a pair of socks, made up the bed, then returned downstairs and poured himself a second cup of coffee before reaching for the phone. Leaning back in the kitchen chair, he punched in Claire's number, frustrated to find his call going to her answering machine.

If you leave your name and number, I promise to—

She must still be in bed. A night owl, Claire liked to work late into the night when she couldn't sleep. She often slept late in the morning, offering her clients afternoon or early evening appointments.

John emptied the cats' litter box, then tried to phone Lydia again, and then Claire once more, exasperated by his failure to reach either of them. For the first time in his life, it occurred to him that it might be a good idea to start seeing a therapist, if only he could find one as smart and insightful as Claire.

He was not, as a rule, an impulsive man, but right then and there decided to drive down to Claire's without letting her know he was coming. Although she seldom answered the phone in the morning, she was sure to be up by the time he got there. He could only hope she would make allowances for this early, possibly inconvenient, visit.

He was ready to leave the house when Lydia unexpectedly phoned from her hospital bed, leaving no doubt that this was going to be another trying day, possibly even more so than yesterday. Half an hour later, John's bandaged hand was still throbbing and, to make matters worse, he discovered something wrong with his BMW. The car felt sluggish and rough today, and kept misfiring each time he tried to accelerate. He suspected it was nothing more serious than faulty spark plugs, but all the same was aggrieved by the bad timing, as if some divine power had decided to keep testing his mettle.

Everything had been going wrong since yesterday, when St. Margaret's Hospital called with the devastating news. His thoughts kept returning to Lydia, who, he feared, might never recover from yet another loss. She had a history of impetuous decisions in times of acute distress. Years ago, following her abortion, she suddenly decided to register for a Cordon Bleu course in Ottawa, two hours away! Much later, a week after her miscarriage, she informed him she wanted to adopt a child. They argued about it for the next few days—which was, he would later think, precisely what she wanted, for it had evidently taken her mind off her chaotic grief.

A mild depression followed, lasting for at least two months. But when, at his wits' end, John finally relented about the adoption, Lydia changed her mind, saying she wasn't sure she could love a stranger's child after all.

All this came back to John on his way to Old Montreal, as he sat in the car, waiting for a traffic light. Although Lydia had phoned only to ask one question that morning, their brief conversation ended up compounding his distress. He needed Claire more than ever now. It occurred to him that, for all he knew, at that very moment, some indifferent stranger was cremating his only child.

Emmanuel Gabriel.

The name was his father's and would have been his son's, but this was the first time John allowed his mind to dwell on it since receiving news of the stillbirth. Though uttered only inwardly, the name sent a bolt of pain through his exhausted body. He thanked his stars for his unexpected involvement with Claire, whose professional training made her singularly qualified to help with marital issues.

She must have been having coffee at the window and seen him park across the street. She was waiting for him at the open door, watching him step out of the elevator. He strode down the long, carpeted corridor, tight-lipped, running a nervous hand through his hair. Claire stood motionless on the threshold, frowning a little. Still in her bathrobe, she was free of makeup and wearing eyeglasses instead of her usual contact lenses. She was not the sort of woman who enjoyed surprises, but had quickly perceived that something exceptional must have happened.

"What is it?" Her eyes scanned his bandaged hand, his drawn, ashen face. "What happened to you?" Gone was the playful, ironic look she often wore when she greeted him. She moved closer and placed her cool fingers on his arm, peering into his eyes. "John—?"

"It was stillborn," he said in a hollow voice. He closed the door, hesitated, and, suddenly weak-kneed, leaned his back against it.

And then, at last, he began to weep.

9

Dr. Seager had just left when Lydia impulsively decided to phone her husband, hoping to catch him before he left home for the day. It was early Tuesday morning, her second day at St. Margaret's maternity ward.

"What are they going to do with him?" she let out the moment John picked up the phone.

"Do with him?" he echoed. Though she had caught him on his way out, he sounded patient but utterly exhausted. She could clearly visualize his expression as he struggled with the words. "Cremate him, I guess."

"What, you're not sure?" Lydia shifted her weight in the firm hospital bed. "Didn't you ask?"

"Yes," he said. "I've signed release forms. I hope that's all right with you."

"What do you mean all right?"

He said, "I mean my taking care of...you know, all the formalities." He cleared his throat. "They said it had to be done...yesterday."

A small, incoherent sound escaped Lydia. "So, he's going to be cremated today?"

"I believe so. I hope that's all right," he repeated.

"What do you mean all right? Was there anything else we could have done?"

"Well." She heard him sigh into the telephone. "We could've had a burial, I suppose."

"Burial," she echoed, like a foreigner practising a new word. "You mean a regular funeral, a gravestone?"

"I suppose," he said. "Some people do choose this option but—"

She broke in, breathless with confusion. "Would I be able to attend?"

"I don't know. It would depend...you'd have to ask your doctor."

"He could've had a gravestone," she said musingly. "I could've gone to visit."

John said, "Oh, Lydia, darling!" Then, "It's not as if—"

But she broke in with sudden heat. "You could've asked me, couldn't you? I'm his mother! The least you could've done was ask me!"

"I'm sorry, my dear," he said, "but...I wanted to spare you, I—" There was a brief pause, then he went on more briskly. "I thought you weren't ready...that it would be thoughtless of me. You understand that, don't you?"

Lydia said nothing, letting out a small, incoherent sound.

"Please don't come today," she finally said.

"What?" said her husband. "What do you mean don't come?"

She closed her eyes. "I mean I don't want to see you...not today. I need to be alone right now. Please." She swallowed hard, then, without waiting for him to answer, hung up the phone and pressed her face against the moist pillow, doing her best to abdicate thought.

10

"The truth is I did not really want the baby," John Gabriel said, fumbling for his pipe. He had at some point tried to give up smoking but found himself, like his father, attached to his pipe habit. "At least...I don't know. I'm not sure I did."

It was by now late morning. Claire had insisted he lie down for a while, and he drifted off while she made some calls in her home office. But now they were both seated in the living room, facing her fireplace. The weather remained fickle. It had been briefly sunny a little earlier, but now rain was coming down again, making dull, slapping sounds as it struck the windows. The fire hissed and crackled, spitting out an occasional spark.

John took a sip of coffee, then set the mug down on the coffee table. It was a large marble table cluttered with books and two small bronze sculptures. There was a pile of *New Yorker* magazines and, resting on top of it, a packet of weed.

"I've never been so confused," John said, drawing on his pipe. "I keep thinking that—"

He hesitated, nervously licking his cracked lower lip. Claire was staring at him over the rim of her coffee mug. "What? You think you willed it to happen?"

This was the sort of insight that occasionally made Claire seem positively psychic; the way his mother used to seem when he was a child.

"Yes," he finally said, "Exactly." He shifted his weight on the olive-hued sofa, crossing his legs. "At the same time, I keep doubting myself. I wonder, you know: could my not wanting the child, my thinking that I didn't want it, have been a purely defensive mechanism?"

He paused, his eyes landing on an intriguing Italian lithograph hanging next to the fireplace. Had he been unconsciously protecting himself against disappointment, against another potential miscarriage?

"I just don't know. I wish I could be sure," he said.

Claire was silent, lost in thought. She was leaning back in one of the wing chairs, staring into the fire. John sipped his coffee. Out of sheer habit, he checked his watch, then frowned at his wounded hand. It could have been worse. He might have sustained permanent damage to his fingers and been forced to abandon his surgical career. The thought made him feel sick to his stomach.

"What really bothers me," he said after a while, "is the inability to interpret my own motives. Even my own desires! I've always thought I knew myself pretty well."

"And so you do," said Claire. "Insofar as it's possible for any man to be objective about himself." She looked at him with a complicated expression, fiddling with her turtleneck. She had, after he lay down, put on a pair of jeans and a blue pullover that had the effect of making her sage-green eyes look almost blue. She was still looking pensive, her long fingers restless, her head slightly tilted.

"I once read a story," she said at length. "I can't remember the author's name, but I know I still have it—somewhere." She made a vague, sweeping gesture in the direction of her bookcase. "Anyway, the story centred on a brilliant school principal—one of those prestigious American prep schools—who keeps putting off marrying and having children because he's afraid that his progeny might let him down." Claire almost smiled. She had features that never failed to fascinate John, so complex was the range of her facial expressions.

"Why?" he asked now, setting his pipe aside. "He could have married and not had kids? Lots of people do."

"Of course," she said. "But, as it turned out, he had a change of heart. When he was almost on the threshold of old age, he finally got married and even managed to produce a son."

"And?" John picked up his mug. "Did the kid turn out all right?"

"Well, that depends on your point of view. He ended up running a successful filling station in Florida."

"I see!" John made an ambiguous little sound, vaguely wishing Claire would raise her thermostat. All the Brits he knew kept frigid houses, while he had grown used to much warmer interiors, if only because both his mother and his wife hated chilly rooms.

"If parents could have a crystal ball, I daresay few of them would choose to have any children."

Claire raised an eyebrow. "You think?"

"I do," John answered. "People expect so much from their offspring and—well, one way or another, most of them end up feeling disappointed, don't they?"

"Hm." Claire crossed her legs, pondering the question. "I suppose as an investment in the future, parenthood *is* a rather risky business." Her gaze wandered toward a framed photograph of her own grown daughter. There were many photographs in the living room, but her daughter's had pride of place on the mantelpiece.

"So—?" said John.

"So, you tell me." She gave him a steady, clinical look. "Do you suppose something like this was going on with you? That this is what your ambivalence was about?"

"I don't know! That's just what I keep trying to tell you!"

He stopped to mull it over, staring at the sputtering grate. He recalled his initial excitement when he first learned of Lydia's pregnancy, and then his gnawing doubts, the secret apprehensions.

"This is what bothers me, you see. When you open up a patient in the OR, you know—*I* know—where the problem lies, and what I have to do about it, but—" He hesitated, searching for the right words.

"You're finding it harder to figure out what's ailing you?"

"Yes," he said, his eyes fluttering. "Exactly."

She smiled at him, scanning his face with a sort of compassionate sadness. They drank their coffee. Claire fiddled with her silver pendant.

"When did the doubts actually start for you? Do you know?" she asked.

He pondered it for a moment. "I'm not sure," he said, tapping his pipe lightly. "At some point, though, I became aware that I had feelings I couldn't sort out."

He paused again, aware of her narrow eyes studying him. He told her how one day, watching Lydia's brother with his two young sons, it came to him suddenly that, like most people, he himself probably wanted a child for purely selfish reasons.

"What do you mean?" interjected Claire. "Someone to care for you in your old age, or a chance at immortality?"

"Neither, exactly," he said. "More like a chance to redeem my own failures, I think." He shrugged, turning back to face her. His head was starting to pound.

She gave him a searching look, then let out an exaggerated sigh.

"What?" said John.

"I can't quite figure you out," she said at length. She fiddled with an African paper knife, its edge playing against the flesh of her palm. "I can't work out why the word *failure* figures so often in your conversation."

"Does it?" John was genuinely taken aback. "Really?"

She smiled at him wanly. "And I don't understand why. I mean, I know your parents were exceedingly demanding, but—" She spread her long hands. "Here you are: a still-young and attractive man, a widely respected surgeon, yet apparently suffering from some secret sense of failure." She gave him a long, steady gaze. "What's it all about, John?"

He turned this over for a while but ended up losing his train of thought, for just then, his wife's face, as pale and luminous as the moon, floated across his mind, accompanied by her echoing voice. *I don't want to see you today.*

He covered his face with his hands, warding off both voice and image. At length he spoke. "I told you ages ago, I grew up thinking I was second best. I did tell you, didn't I?"

"So you did."

He frowned. His restless gaze, roaming about the room, landed on Claire's daughter, photographed in her school uniform at the age of six. He recalled that Claire would be going away on the weekend, having made plans to celebrate her daughter's nineteenth birthday in Toronto.

His thoughts drifted back to his own distant school days at Lower Canada College; the endless frustration of being the third in his class, never able to surpass a pair of clever Jewish twins at the top. This childhood experience had left him with an ambivalent attitude toward his Jewish colleagues: he both admired and resented them, using them as a measuring stick for his own achievements. It was no accident that he ended up on staff at the Jewish General Hospital.

"Both my parents," he was soon telling Claire, "managed to communicate a subtle but ongoing message: you must try, you must keep doing your best, though we know you will never get to be number one."

As he said this, John felt a stab at his heart, as if the words echoing beyond his memory's door had only that moment been uttered by one of his parents.

"My sister," he said, "had it easier in some ways. She could do anything, could be anything, but her husband had better not be anybody's fool."

A sigh escaped John's throat. Sadly, she had been born plain, he had overheard an aunt say when he was a teenager. Relatives still spoke of his sister in whispers: "Poor Helen—such a clever girl, but so unlucky!"

She was thirty-five, married and divorced twice. There had been physical abuse in the first marriage and homosexual liaisons in the second.

Yet, despite everything, his sister had become a successful journalist. Without fuss or bother, without much parental encouragement, she had gone on to accomplish her own professional goals.

"But they must be proud of you?" Claire was saying. "Your father's some kind of merchant, if I'm not mistaken?"

"A wine importer," said John. "But, yes, they are pretty proud."

"So—?"

"So—" said John. And then he looked up and met her probing eyes and, all at once, felt she was not merely fishing, that she knew what was at the bottom of this deep, murky well. "Has Ken said anything about me?" he asked suddenly.

"About you?" She looked at him with arched eyebrows. Ken was her ex-husband. "He doesn't even know I've been seeing you."

"Is that right?"

"I never kiss and tell," she said and quirked her lips. "Anyway, Ken's got his own highly colourful love life."

"Is yours colourful?"

She returned his smile, though it quickly faded into a look of playful reproach. "Methinks someone is trying to change the subject!"

"Change the subject?" He re-lit his pipe. "What *is* the subject, exactly?"

"The subject—the unanswered question—is: what's making you feel so... inadequate?"

"Inadequate," John echoed, as if trying to remember the precise meaning of a foreign word.

He sat there for a moment, scanning the room. It was a large, airy room full of beautiful objects, but much too cluttered for his own taste. Neither did he share Claire's taste in art, though he was intrigued by the lithograph she had brought back from a recent trip to Florence. It showed two brown-ink figures enclosed in a blurred yellowish circle. The two figures were joined at the back but seemed to be straining away, as if they might fly, or leap, across the yellow boundary.

A deep sigh escaped John's throat. Of course, he knew the answer to Claire's question. What's more, he wished he could unburden himself, though the prospect made a small wave of shame wash over his heart. To think that he could not dismiss thoughts of professional setbacks even now, when his wife lay in hospital, struggling with her grief! He hardly needed his mother-in-law to remind him of Lydia's desperate state, but she happened to call his pager just then, having repeatedly failed to reach her daughter.

John called her back on Claire's phone. He did his best to reassure the poor woman, who sounded barely coherent with worry. He had just spoken to Lydia that morning, he told her, but only very briefly. She was doing reasonably well, he lied. He was going to see her a little later, he added, though in truth he had yet to decide whether or not to honour his wife's explicit wishes to be left alone.

He cleared his throat and promised his mother-in-law he would call her again by the end of the day. Then he hung up and sat rubbing his aching temples, willing himself to put aside his thoughts of Lydia, for whom he felt a chaotic mix of pity, solicitude, resentment. To think that a woman would not want to see her own husband at a time like this! The father of the child she was mourning!

"All right," he finally said to Claire. "All right. Just get me something for my headache, will you? Then I'll tell you…I'll do my best to answer your question."

11

As far back as she could remember, Lydia had longed to know what it would be like to inhabit other people's skin. As a child, she was often accused of having too much imagination. Whenever she encountered an amputee or a lame soldier, or just an ordinary villager with a twitch, she would go about imitating that person for hours, sometimes days, until she felt she knew what it would be like to live with that particular deficit or affliction.

One day, visiting Mytilene, their island's capital, she passed a blind man picking his way through the hectic marketplace and, back home in the village, began to wander through the house with eyes squeezed shut and arms stretched out, feeling her way from room to room.

The extended arms, alas, failed to prevent her from stumbling on one of the steps leading into the garden. She broke her left arm and had to be taken by taxi to a clinic in nearby Kalloni to get a cast put on.

After that, whenever her mother spotted her "trying to be someone God in his infinite wisdom had never meant her to be," an old belt would be promptly brought out, in hopes of beating the devil out of the child.

The belt belonged to Lydia's father, but the punishment was invariably meted out by her mother, herself no stranger to physical abuse, having fallen victim on more than one occasion to her husband's drunken rages.

It was said that being orphaned as a very young boy had left its scars on Phevos Dimou's psyche. Some families were lucky and some unlucky. It was as simple as that. Phevos had lost his parents during the German Occupation, his eldest brother and an uncle during the Civil War. Later, his firstborn son died of the measles at the age of five. There you had it: the ever-present power of the Evil Eye.

The Dimou men were known to have a fiery temperament, yet Phevos, unlike most village fathers, had never so much as spanked his two daughters; once or twice, he had given his younger son a thrashing, but for all his flaws, Lydia's father was deeply loved.

There had been a quirky side to his nature; as a young father, he'd had an aura of perpetual eagerness, as if he might at any moment take it into his head to hop onto a mule's back or dive into the sea. He had been moody all his life, but also droll, energetic, generous. He loved to take his kids to remote beaches, or for long hikes in the mountains, collecting wild greens or berries or snails, thrilling them with wild adventure stories.

But Lydia had always known that her father was unreliable and, unlike the man she would eventually marry, psychologically unstable.

One summer, working in Mytilene, he went with his stonemason cronies for an ouzo and a game of cards in one of the coffee shops. A few days later, he returned to the village, singing. They were all emigrating to Canada, he announced over lunch.

"Canada? Why Canada?" his wife had demanded. "Isn't it very cold there?"

"It's a great country. Very peaceful and rich. I'm going to go alone, then bring the rest of you over."

Antigone crossed herself. *"Panaghia mou!* Have you gone mad, *kale*?"

"Not at all, woman!" In Mytilene, he'd run into a distant cousin whose brother had emigrated and who was now the owner of two successful Montreal eateries. The Mytilene cousin was also ready to leave for Canada. "I've got their address and phone number. I'm going to borrow money and join them as soon as I can," Phevos decided.

And so he did.

A year after he left, a holiday package arrived in the village, with presents for everyone. Lydia's gift was a charming little diary, with pink pages and a golden lock. Having recently turned eleven, she immediately set about filling its crisp pages, launching a personal habit she was to keep up in all the years to come, writing at first in her mother tongue, then at some point switching to English.

Whatever the language, she discovered the joy of recording her adolescent secrets; eventually, too, the unexpected pleasure of giving shape to her innermost thoughts and feelings.

It was something she still enjoyed doing as a married woman but, rushing to St. Margaret's after her water broke, all Lydia could think to grab was her overnight case with its nightgown and bathrobe and slippers. She had not expected her hospital stay to last longer than a day or two at the most. Now, all alone in her bare hospital room, she wished she had the journal so she could at least unburden herself on its pages. She must ask John to bring it next time he comes.

But then she remembered telling him to stay away from her, hanging up on him!

The thought was accompanied by a fresh spurt of tears. At the same time, a long-suppressed idea was starting to clamour for attention. The thought of divorcing John had been there for some time now, hatching behind a closed psychological door. The door was barricaded because, after all, he had done the honourable thing all those years ago; had married her when another man might have dumped her: a poor immigrant's pregnant daughter.

Not only had John stood by her but he had, over the years, encouraged and supported her interests and growth. True, he had urged her to get an abortion the first time she found herself pregnant, but he had been just a junior resident at the time, and they had not yet known each other all that well.

Lydia drifted off again, then woke up in a darkening room to the clap of thunder. It was not yet three p.m. but raining hard—raining cats and dogs, as her mother liked to say, with palpable relish, once she'd learned what the expression meant.

The memory brought a familiar ache to Lydia's chest. She thought of her mother's struggles with Canadian weather and strangers who did not speak her language, her bewilderment whenever her three children came home with a new idiom.

"Why do Canadians stick dogs into everything?" she had asked one day when they were all in the kitchen, eating hot dogs and fries. "Food, houses, weather! Why dogs?"

"Well," Lydia recalled asking. "Why does it rain chair legs in Greek?"

They laughed at that. Lydia, who had been admitted to the International School of Montreal, was quickly becoming fluent in both French and English, but, as a grown woman, would tell her friends that her soul would remain Greek to the day she died. She would have been hard put to define "soul" but found it intriguing that, after all these years in Canada, she often spoke to herself in her mother tongue and that so many of her deepest thoughts were anchored in her beloved Aegean village.

12

Although she had managed to produce an elegant meal for their first dinner, Claire claimed to be bored by routine cooking and, it appeared, shopping for food as well. True, she had not expected him to show up this morning, John reminded himself, but how you could end up with nothing in your fridge but artichokes, bread, and two cucumbers was a bit beyond him.

Not that he really cared about any of that right now. He had no more appetite than he'd had yesterday, yet he couldn't help thinking of Lydia, who was an excellent cook and who—perhaps due to hunger in early childhood—never felt secure unless their fridge and freezer were overflowing.

He had called his wife twice, but she would not answer, so he finally gave up and called his office, then agreed to have lunch with Claire, such as it was.

He had not intended to spend so much time with her, but then Claire often made him do things he'd had no intention of doing. Watching her go at a steamed artichoke, her sharp, square teeth extracting every bit of green flesh from the stiff petals, it occurred to him that she brought the same concentration, the same lofty patience, to everything she took on, including his own troubles. The problem was that he often found himself scraping up far more than he had bargained for.

All the same, he was glad, even relieved, to be able to air his private anguish, the one disappointment he'd had to learn to live with, like some of his own inoperable patients. Yes, he was a surgeon; he was competent, he was presentable, he was respected by his colleagues. He could have gone on with the list without, he thought, undue self-regard. Only he was, and would always remain, just another general surgeon while someone else, someone he ran into nearly every day, had taken over the retired Surgeon-in-Chief's office.

The lingering bitterness both pained and embarrassed him, if only because he could not, just then, help thinking of his wife and her infinitely greater suffering. His petty concerns brought on a wave of inner shame but did not stop him from trying to explain his feelings.

"It wouldn't be so bad," he told Claire, "if it had been an older guy. But Gurman and I went through med school together and, you know how it is, everybody knew it was him or me—I mean, even before Abramson had retired."

And then one day, he suddenly understood it would not be him. Only with the greatest of efforts did John manage to look up from his plate and meet Claire's searching gaze.

"What made you so sure?"

"What made me so sure? It's quite simple—and understandable, to be fair. It's a Jewish hospital. Syd Gurman is Jewish. I'm sure the Greeks would have done the same." He looked down at his coffee-stained bandage, wishing he could shake the feeling that, one way or another, he had been wronged. "Of course, they wouldn't say so," he added. "They made a big deal out of Gurman's research."

Claire licked her glistening mouth. "I'm sorry," she eventually said, "I don't think you are right about the Jewish factor. Certainly not these days. Anyway, hasn't research always been an important consideration?"

"Oh," John said. "It is—it certainly is—but Gurman's never amounted to all that much. What's more," he went on, "I happen to be a better surgeon—I don't think I'm flattering myself—I think Ken would confirm it if you were to ask him." He gave a small, self-deprecating shrug. "The problem is I haven't done any research."

"And why not?"

"I'd planned to—I did try," John answered. "I was interested in colorectal cancer techniques, but...

well, the fact is I couldn't get the funding." He sat up and squared his shoulders, feeling the throb of his lingering headache. "The MRC turned down my grant application."

This admission cost John considerable effort, though he believed the rejection was almost certainly due to his mediocre writing skills and lack of experience in preparing a grant application. Should he have asked a more experienced colleague to review the application before submitting it? Had he been too proud to do so?

Claire gazed at him with vague commiseration. "I'm told lots of people fail to get funding these days—?"

"Oh, sure," John said, "and they're all miserable. Anyway, I'm not used to being rejected, I guess."

When the decision had come from the MRC, he could hardly believe it. "Everyone got to hear about it—the surgeons, nurses, even the secretaries." He paused, averting his eyes. "I had to say—I don't know how many times before it was finally over—*No, I didn't get it*. To put up with their fucking sympathy. Sympathy! *No, I was turned down.* It's not easy to say, you know? Not while others you work with—Gurman, for one—walk around with their smug, superior smiles."

All this was rehashed over their cucumber-sandwich lunch. John wiped his mouth and rose to get his pipe, taken aback by his own reflection in Claire's antique mirror.

That this gaunt, tight-lipped man with his greying hair and resolute chin should be him! Dr. John Gabriel: a man ambushed by time, he found himself thinking. Next week, he would be turning forty and it all seemed to have fallen short somehow.

"I must be going through some sort of mid-life crisis," he told Claire, returning to the table. He was vaguely impressed by his own ability to admit this, but when he looked up again, it was to find Claire wearing one of her ironic smiles.

"Am I one of the symptoms then? Of your mid-life crisis?" she asked, her tongue sliding across her lower lip. She had a rather long mouth with a full lower lip and small pearly teeth. She grinned and her mouth gleamed at him.

"If it is a symptom, it's a highly agreeable one," he said gallantly.

But perhaps she had hoped for a different declaration, for her face grew abruptly serious, her back straight with purpose. She smoked in silence for a moment or two, while John fiddled with his hand-carved pipe.

"I've been wondering," she said at length. "Does Lydia know how unhappy you've been about Abramson's position?"

"No," John said. "I never got around to telling her, I'm afraid."

"Oh?" Claire exhaled. "Why ever not? Did you think Lydia too would look down her nose at you?"

"No, no, nothing like that!" said John, feeling a little miffed. "On the contrary, she would have just—oh, you know, pooh-poohed the whole thing. She'd have said what did it matter—I love doing surgery after all. I do."

John sat for a moment, musing on something Lydia had told him in bed one day. She had been reading a book on insanity, laughing to learn that, in early nineteenth century France, there had reportedly been a madman known as Diogenes, a solitary individual who had been institutionalized for running through the streets of Paris in a Greek costume, claiming he had been charged with the philosophical mission of curing humanity of ambition.

Lydia had loved the story, but John recalled that he himself had only rolled his eyes when she stopped to share it with him. Though he had persuaded his wife to enroll full time at university after they returned from their Greek honeymoon, and despite her eventual Honours degree, she had always seemed to him surprisingly lacking in ambition. He had urged her to go to graduate school, which might have opened up full-time career opportunities, but Lydia demurred, seemingly content with her part-time copy editor's job. Had she simply been biding her time, hoping to stay home eventually, and raise a family?

"Anyway," he said to Claire, "I had every intention of telling her about it. In fact, I really wanted to."

"But—?"

"But—well, it so happened that Lydia had just found out she was finally pregnant. I didn't want to be a spoilsport, I guess."

"I see." said Claire, looking up from her cup of coffee.

"Yes," John said vaguely. "And so there I was...sick with professional disappointment, while she—well, all she seemed interested in just then was the baby, the baby!" His voice, he realized, had grown thin on the two last words. "Oh, you know," he said in an altered tone, "you know how women get when they're pregnant. They become one-track-minded, don't they?" He shrugged, then hastened to add, "It's natural, of course. I realize that. Were you like that too?" he asked, trying for a smile.

But the question remained unanswered.

"You sound angry," Claire said after a thoughtful moment. "But in all fairness, you can't reproach Lydia. She didn't know about the Surgeon-in-Chief position, did she?" Before John could respond, she added, "As I see it, you chose to shut her out, then became unreasonably resentful at finding yourself alone with your misery." She met his eyes across the dining table. "Have I got it right?"

"Yes...look, I know I was being childish—I really do—but imagine yourself in my shoes," said John, "having to sit through dinner listening to her chatter about cribs and prenatal classes while I...I was in pain, I tell you. So, yes. Yes, rightly or wrongly, I suppose I did feel somewhat resentful." He looked at her for a moment, swallowing hard. "I sound like a real jerk, don't I? It's unfair. I *know* it's unfair. I didn't want to tell her how hurt I was, but all the same, I must have wanted to be mothered just then...a little."

"Mothered." Claire said. "Very interesting."

John made a small scoffing sound. "Just a figure of speech, Dr. Freud."

Claire offered no answer. She appeared lost in thought, while John smoked his pipe, aware of renewed scratchiness in the back of his throat. Both his wife and his mistress thought him a bit of a hypochondriac. Doctors, he had overheard Lydia say to his own sister, made the worst patients.

A moment or two went by. John dabbed at his nostrils, glancing at Claire, who was, as so often, looking inscrutable. Her summer-bronzed face, with its high cheekbones and narrow eyes, gave away nothing, except perhaps a glimmer of some private amusement.

"Have you ever had a mistress before?" she suddenly asked.

"What? No!" he said, then stopped, surprised by his own tone: he'd sounded almost offended, like a man who would never so much as consider looking at another woman. *Not just a jerk but a hypocrite!* "No," he repeated, looking away. "I'm obviously not quite the man I thought I was," he added judiciously.

"Hm," said Claire. After a while, she turned and stared out the tall windows. It was raining now. John asked for coffee, then found himself engulfed by a fresh wave of shame: that he should allow himself to wallow in self-pity while his poor wife lay in a hospital bed, alone with her private anguish.

He consulted his watch. "Oh, never mind," he said, remembering a post-op patient he needed to check up on. "Let's forget the coffee. I think I'd better go now."

But all he really wanted was to be able to go back to bed and sleep for the rest of the day.

13

After her husband's death, Lydia's mother had become progressively unreliable. Her memory, her judgment, seemed so radically altered that John had at some point begun to suspect the onset of early Alzheimer's. Lydia had vehemently rejected the very suggestion. It was nothing but grief and panic, she had argued not so long ago.

The telephone conversation she'd just had with her mother, though, left her wondering whether her husband might have been right after all. Her mother reported talking to John earlier but what she said to Lydia now barely made sense.

"I know it's not your fault. It's him, isn't it?" her mother said, clicking her tongue. "I know he won't let you wear it, I know that—"

Lydia would not let her finish. "Oh, not that again, Mama!"

So that's what it was all about: the Evil Eye amulet she'd refused to wear all through her pregnancy, making her mother fervently cross herself.

Lydia took a long steadying breath. "Please, Mama, you know perfectly well I agree with John," she said, speaking patiently but feeling utterly hopeless. "How many times have I told you? We both think it's utter nonsense."

But her mother only sighed into the phone and, with typical Greek resignation, concluded there was nothing to be done anyway.

"He's an educated man, what can you expect? You have to take the good with the bad, my daughter."

An ambulance approached the hospital with its siren blaring; Antigone's voice faded briefly, then re-surfaced. "At least yours doesn't drink, and he earns good money. Doesn't chase skirts either. They all want to tell you what to do though, don't they?"

"Maybe so," said Lydia. She spoke wearily, swept by desolation over her earlier churlishness with her husband. She felt sure that he was doing his best. So obviously trying to please her. Guilt was starting to gnaw at the contours of her heart.

All the same, she was still not ready to see family or friends. Her mother-in-law had sent a beautiful bouquet of gladiolus, but Lydia had pleaded with John to make sure that his parents stayed away for now.

The only relative she might have liked to see was John's sister, who was travelling in Mexico, covering a story for the CBC. Lydia thought: too bad; someone to take my side in that family. John's parents, his relatives, would all be talking. Discussing her lost baby. Her failure. Whatever they said, whatever they thought, only Helen could be counted on to stand up for her.

Like a ponderous, wounded animal, Lydia slid off the bed and inched her way toward the bathroom, seized by fresh despair.

She could hardly blame John if he decided never to come at all. She had always been the sort of person who liked to be left alone when she was sick. Would he remember that, though? Except during PMS, she had rarely been unwell. But now, instead of a baby, all she had to carry around was a urine drainage bag, attached to her body by a long, plastic cord. Every time she got off the bed, it was there, pinned to her hospital gown, getting heavier.

She was still sitting on the toilet when she heard a knock on the bathroom door.

"Mrs. Gabriel?"

A foghorn voice, a German accent. Lydia's grandparents had starved to death in their Aegean village; she had been raised in the shadow of the German occupation, her father's lifelong loathing.

"I'll...be out in a minute."

"May I come in?"

"Pardon?"

"Let me help you...don't worry, it's our job, you know."

"Thank you, but…I'm almost finished," Lydia said, thinking: How normal my voice sounds—docile, polite, as if this were just a routine medical visit.

Her face stared back at her in the mirror, colourless as dough. An ageless face framed by wild curls; a stranger's eyes, large and dim and inscrutable. She unlocked the door.

"I'm Miss Koch." The nurse came around the supply cart, a squat, stern-faced woman with grey hair and darting eyes that landed, briefly, on Lydia's bloated belly. She helped her back onto the bed.

"Did you have a bowel movement?"

"Yes…sort of. The laxative helped a little. I still can't pee on my own though." She dropped her gaze, staring at the transparent drainage bag.

"Well, it's nothing to be ashamed of; it's what catheters are for." The nurse went about swabbing the wounded flesh: quickly, efficiently. "Am I hurting you?" Despite her efforts at self-control, Lydia had moaned.

"A little," she said, thinking in Greek: *Ach, panaghia mou!*

She shut her eyes, her mind darting from the plastic bag swelling with her own urine to the God who, for nearly two decades, she'd claimed not to believe in. Bitterness shook her insides. Her suppressed anger—at herself, her husband, at Koch—had abruptly shifted to God. For surely there was a God? Surely there was some overwhelming reason?

"That's all, you see?" It was all over. Her bladder was empty now; her womb empty, too, though, so far as she could tell, her abdomen seemed hardly, if at all, diminished.

"I've got bad cramps again," she said with a sudden grimace. Miss Koch was thrusting her hand into her hollow flesh, pressing below the navel.

"Don't worry. I'll give you a painkiller." She guided Lydia's hand. "You must help your uterus get back to normal." She thrust a thermometer under Lydia's tongue, then paused long enough to take her blood pressure. "I'm sorry about your baby," she said suddenly.

Lydia looked up, taken aback by the altered tone. Miss Koch's raisin-like eyes blinked briefly into hers. She felt her own blur with tears. "Thank you."

"On a scale of one to ten, how bad is the pain?"

"I don't know," said Lydia. "Maybe seven or eight?"

Miss Koch handed her a little paper cup with a couple of tiny pills.

"This will soon fix that—it may make you a little groggy though." The nurse discarded the cup, taking in Lydia's untouched lunch tray. There was the hospital food, as well as homemade delicacies her mother had managed to send with her caretaker. "You didn't eat anything," she noted. "Would you like me to help you?"

"Not right now. Thank you."

"Well, never mind, there's nothing like a snooze on a rainy day, is there?"

Lydia nodded. Flashes of lightning ripped the sky, illuminating the dreary room. She found herself wishing that she were back in her own home, in her cozy solarium, where she had her aquarium, her tropical plants and blooming orchids. It was here that she liked to read or write in her journal, watching the seasons change.

Then she thought of the beautiful nursery they'd prepared for the baby, and found herself recalling how, back in their village, her mother would collect rose petals—red and yellow velvet fallen from their own bushes—and boil them on their gas range, then, when it cooled, use the concentrated liquid as eyewash after a crying spell.

Lydia was not sure how old she'd been when she first watched her mother do it, but eventually observed that it usually happened whenever her father drank; when he lost a job or money, playing cards in the *kapheneion*. That was how, from an early age, Lydia learned to associate the fragrance of roses with her mother's pain.

14

"Oh, fuck!"

Dr. John Gabriel had just stepped off the elevator and was about to leave his office building when he realized that it was pouring outside and his umbrella was in the car. It was a large, windproof umbrella, purchased in London by his roving sister. Right now, though, this fine umbrella was in the back of his BMW. The car was in a repair shop, though the problem had turned out to be minor: he had been right about the spark plugs. The rain went on hurling down Côte-des-Neiges Road.

Sighing, John stopped to consult his watch. He dithered at the entrance, next to an X-ray technician who had telephoned for a taxi. There was a taxi stand one block down, but no cab seemed to be coming.

A second elevator arrived, ejecting a handful of patients and chattering office workers. His receptionist was among them, dressed in bright green vinyl and a matching rain hat. A black-clad Hasid stomped in from the rain, clutching a floral bouquet, shaking his wet umbrella. John was reminded that he'd meant to buy roses for Lydia, though he wasn't sure she would even let him get past the threshold, flowers or no flowers. It occurred to him that he should have tried to call her again, if only to see whether her mood had changed.

For a moment John Gabriel stared at the rain pounding the sidewalk, shaking his head in muddled despair. He tried to control his nerves, but without much success. His headache was back. His bandaged hand was still throbbing. He drew a deep breath. *Relax, relax, relax.*

A quarter of an hour went by. The rain began to let up—enough, at any rate, for him to venture making it to his mechanic's garage without getting soaked. The shop was two blocks away from his office; he could do it in five minutes if he ran.

And so he did but, the weather being especially prankish that day, the light drizzle abruptly turned into another downpour. He was drenched and foul-tempered by the time he arrived at St. Margaret's. He stepped into the lobby, shivering, relieved to find a bouquet of white rosebuds at the hospital's gift shop. The last one. As he was leaving, he spotted a decorative urn by the window and, inwardly stirred, thought this was probably what he would have to buy for his son's ashes. He must come back tomorrow, before Lydia was ready to be discharged.

The thought brought on a dart of pain, hastily pushed aside. He was relieved not to have to go looking for an urn, but even more so to find his wife acting as if nothing untoward had taken place between them. Lydia seemed taken aback when he came into the room, but possibly only because of his dishevelled appearance.

She sat up the moment he closed the door, her eyes widening. She urged him to drape his wet clothes over the radiators and put on her bathrobe. Her robe was pink and barely covered his knees but he obeyed without protest.

She stared at him for a moment before speaking. "You look like a dog caught in a rainstorm."

She almost achieved a smile.

15

They lived in Upper Outremont, in a spacious Georgian house purchased with an inheritance from John's childless uncle. Lydia had been twenty-six when they first went to see the house, already anxious about her failure to conceive in the past three years. She fell in love with the beautiful English garden but thought the house was much too large for them. Two full floors, five bedrooms, and a third-floor attic.

"What'll I do with all these rooms?" she recalled asking. They had up to then lived in modest one- or two-bedroom apartments.

John liked the house on sight, pointing out its many advantages to a doubtful Lydia. It was a short drive away from both the hospital and his private office and, as it happened, within walking distance of her parents' apartment. This was why she finally decided to dismiss her reservations. She had always wanted to be near her family, but there was no question of actually living any closer with an up-and-coming surgeon for a husband.

Her brother and sister had not yet left home at the time; they were living with their parents on a short, nondescript street off Park Avenue. Most Greeks had moved on over the years, but Lydia's mother still lived in her old, shabby apartment. After her husband died, her three children urged her to move, but Antigone Dimou would not hear of it. Her husband was dead, her children gone. This, she insisted, was where Phevos' memory was still alive. The Upper Outremont home, which Lydia had gradually come to love, was spacious enough to comfortably accommodate her mother, but they all knew that John would have only grudgingly agreed to such a living arrangement, common though it might be in Greek families.

Lydia was deeply attached to her mother, but she understood why John had little patience for her. She could read it in his face even now, as she told him about her mother's telephone call. She had long since given up trying to change her husband's ambivalent feelings toward her family. The success of a marriage, she had at some point come to realize, was largely contingent on the partners' willingness not to ask for more than could be delivered.

"There's something I need to tell you," she said after a while, casting aside her worries about her mother. John was sitting in the only chair, looking like a rumpled dog.

"Tell me." He spoke very gently.

Lydia shifted her gaze, letting it land on the bouquet of roses he'd brought, placing them in a vase he got at the nursing station. "The milk's starting to come, John. It hurts...my whole body's sore, but—" Her voice faltered. "I never thought—no one told me there would be milk anyway."

John exhaled. "They should have," he said. "They'll probably give you anti-lactation pills," he added after a moment. "Have you told the doctor?"

"No." She swiped at her eyes. "I didn't...realize what was happening, not immediately." Her tears were unstoppable. She lay feeling drained and hopeless, focused on her husband's face. He had come to sit on the edge of her bed, taking her hand in his.

"What are they going to do with the ashes?" she asked.

"You—I'm sure they'll let us keep them. I'll get us...a nice urn. Don't worry about any of it," he hastened to add. She saw him check his watch and knew he needed to leave. He'd told her he had promised to drop in on his parents, who lived all the way in Laval.

"Maybe you should go now," she said after a while. "You need to get a good night's sleep after getting soaked like this." She shifted her weight, glancing toward the window. "Looks like it's going to start pouring again."

John made a vaguely resigned gesture. "Is there anything I can get you? Shall I bring you a fresh nightie maybe?"

"No," she said. Then, "Yes, why don't you—not a nightie though. I'd like my pyjamas, please."

"All right," he said. "I'll bring them tomorrow." He rose to check his clothes.

"You mustn't get sick," said Lydia, following him with her eyes. "Take a zinc lozenge tonight. And make sure you don't forget to eat."

"I won't." He sighed, adding: "How's the food here by the way? Are you eating?"

"A little," she said. "Oh, God...I forgot to ask. Did you feed the cats?"

"Yes, of course," he said.

"And the fish?"

"Oh, the fish! I'm so sorry: I forgot the fish!"

She was silent for a moment. "The plants will need watering too. Do you think you could—?" They had an aquarium in the solarium, and a lot of plants. He had never been in the habit of helping around the house.

"Of course," he said. "Please don't worry. I'll take care of everything."

16

A great crashing sound awakened John Gabriel in the middle of the night, followed by a wild screech, then a long, vociferous wail. Sitting bolt upright, his heart thudding, he blinked against the bedside light, his momentary confusion compounded by the presence of Claire, who was sitting in bed next to him, reading a book. She had on a black negligee, but he was wearing only his boxers and undershirt. He could hardly remember the last time they'd had sex, but this was the first full night they had ever spent together. There had been a thunderstorm earlier but that was not what had woken John up. It was barely raining now.

He had come straight from his parents' house, unable to bear the thought of going back to his empty house. He had not planned to spend the night with Claire but, after two stiff drinks, would have been a fool to risk driving home in the furious rainstorm that had started sometime before midnight.

Claire smiled down at him over her reading glasses. "It's nothing," she said. "A feline gang war down in the back alley."

"What time is it?" He heaved himself up, moistening his lips with his tongue. Claire's bedroom seemed very dry, probably because he was used to sleeping with a humidifier.

"A quarter to two."

"Jesus. Why are you still up?" He rubbed his brow. There was a pulsing sensation just below his hairline. In eleven years of marriage, he had slept only a few times without Lydia, all of them while attending surgical conferences.

"I couldn't sleep," said Claire.

"Oh." John shifted uncomfortably. There was another blood-curdling wail from the alley. Sighing, he sank back against the pillows and closed his eyes, the feuding cats sending his thoughts flying back to his long-ago honeymoon in Lydia's ancestral home. How vividly he remembered it all: the beautiful seaside village with its cobblestoned streets and olive orchards, the packs of wretched stray cats wherever they went to eat.

They'd been staying with Lydia's widowed uncle, sleeping on the second floor of an old stone house, when John was jolted out of his dreams by the eeriest sounds he had ever heard. Leaping out of bed, he overturned a lamp on the bedside table. Lydia rolled over and muttered something but went right on sleeping. John was still trying to get his bearings when her widowed uncle came storming up from the downstairs bedroom. It was not yet dawn.

"What's going on?" John had stepped out into the hallway, scratching his head.

"I don't know," the old man said. "I thought I heard something break in your room just now."

"The lamp fell...it didn't break," said John. "What's going on down there?" He stood barefoot in the shadowy hallway, shivering a little.

"Oh!" said the old man. "You mean the cats? A neighbour's sons broke a window, playing ball, and now a cat's given birth in the cellar." He patted John's arm. "Go back to bed. It's still early."

The next morning, they were offered a more elaborate explanation.

Every spring, hundreds of female cats fought ferocious battles against marauding toms. They gave birth in sheltered places: cellars, privies, abandoned houses. Wherever it was, the toms sniffed them out and, after nightfall, went about killing as many newborns as they could. The females did their best to protect the kittens, but, more often than not, lost the battle, and sometimes body parts as well.

All this John and Lydia learned over a prolonged outdoor breakfast, sitting under a grapevine-laced trellis. "Imagine that," John said, speaking in his halting Greek. "That must be how they control population growth."

"Oh, no, no." Lydia's uncle laughed. "It's got nothing to do with that!" The tomcats, he said, killed the kittens so the mothers would go into heat again. "As long as they nurse, the mothers are not interested in making any more babies!" The uncle chuckled, grinning over his small cup of coffee.

Later that afternoon, as they sat in the garden again, a ginger female cat crept out through the broken cellar window, transporting a dead kitten between her teeth. Seeing them, she paused to survey the scene, then loped among the fruit-laden trees, quickly disappearing over the stone fence.

"She's going to bury it," said Lydia, her eyes welling.

"That's nature for you." Her uncle shrugged. "What can you do, eh?"

All this floated through John's mind while he tried to make himself comfortable next to Claire's body. It struck him then that no matter what mental path he happened to be on, awake or asleep, alone or with Claire, sooner or later his thoughts would meander back to his wife.

"Would you like some chamomile tea?" asked Claire, tossing her book aside.

"Yes, please." He sat up, tasting his dry mouth. "Actually, I think I'd prefer something cold," he said. "How about some of your white port?"

"Sure." She fumbled for her slippers.

"With ice, please. I don't know why I'm so thirsty tonight."

He rose to go to the bathroom, then came back, rolling his stiff shoulders. Claire's bed was a beautiful antique brass, but the mattress was much too firm for him. He propped himself against the pillows, sipping his chilled port.

"How can you sleep on this mattress night after night?" he asked after a while. "It's like a bed of bricks."

She flashed him a sidelong grin. "Helps me keep my regal posture."

"Is that so?" John thought of his mother, who was always nagging his sister about improving her posture.

Claire said, "A penny for your thoughts, darling."

John, joggling the melting cubes in his glass, realized he must have sighed. He did not like it when Claire called him "darling."

"I was just thinking of my mother," he said, setting his glass down on the bedside table. "She's so judgmental...clever and competent but too critical. Lydia doesn't want to see her right now, so my mother is offended. She doesn't understand the effect she has on others."

"Oh?" Claire took a last swig from her Scotch.

"Are you sure you want to hear all this now? It's not very interesting."

"Who wants interesting at this hour?" She wrinkled her nose playfully. "Roll over. I'll massage your back while you try to bore me to sleep, how's that?"

"Well...okay." He made a small, ambiguous noise, then did as instructed, going on to talk about his mother's disapproval of Lydia, her subtle condescension toward his wife's family.

"My mother—I hate to say it, I really do—but she's not, when you come right down to it, all that different from my mother-in-law. Lydia's mother may be suffering from incipient Alzheimer's but when I think about them, their younger selves, I see the same Greek village mentality."

John paused, sighed, then waved it all away. He was starting to feel drowsy again. "You give a great massage," he said, turning to kiss her hand.

The gesture was misconstrued. Smiling, Claire leaned in and placed her mouth on his. She kissed him expertly, lingeringly, but, as it turned out, with little effect. The image of his grieving wife made John's body recoil.

"It's no good," he said, putting out his hand to stroke her pale cheekbone. "What I desperately need right now is sleep." He looked at her wryly. "Uninterrupted by cat wars."

"Well, I make no promises about that," she said, "but okay, let's give it a try."

Claire slid down in the bed and pulled up the

duvet, turning her back. It was by now going on four a.m. From the alley came the cry of a stray kitten, mewing pathetically. John shifted his weight, vexed with himself for having agreed to spend the night on this stony mattress. But the iced port seemed to be taking effect and, at length, he felt himself being towed toward the shores of sleep. The kitten went on crying, but he could no longer hear it.

WEDNESDAY
September 4, 1991

17

It is not true that time cures everything. All time does is teach you to live with invisible scars, Lydia found herself thinking. Forty-eight hours after her hospital admission, she could not believe the time would ever come when she would wake up in the morning and be free of the grip of pain, or guilt, or doubt.

"You're not responsible," Dr. Seager had tried to tell her. He had come back to see her first thing that morning, had quickly examined her, then lingered on the edge of her bed, listening, while she forced herself to voice something that had been nagging at her drowsy consciousness. Back in December, as yet unaware that she was pregnant, she'd had too much to drink on at least two occasions.

"I mean, it was Christmas, and then, of course, New Year's Eve," she told the doctor. "My period had always been erratic, so I didn't know. It didn't even—" She stopped. She raised both her hands and, trembling, brought them to her eyes.

Dr. Seager let out an audible sigh. "You must stop blaming yourself," he repeated. There was nothing she could have done—or not done. Nature was sometimes cruel. Unfortunately, her body was still recovering from the recent trauma. She would not be going home yet, as she had been led to expect.

"Try to focus on resting and getting better," he said just before he left.

She was still thinking about the doctor's words, still quietly crying, when someone touched her shoulder. She was lying on her side, her face to the window.

"Mrs. Gabriel?"

Lydia caught her breath. "May I please have a box of tissues…and a painkiller?" she said, face buried in the pillow. She had always hated to cry in the presence of strangers. The wind bellowed outside, tossing heavy raindrops against the shivering glass.

"Yes—I'll get you the nurse in a minute. We…just thought you might like to have this."

The photograph!

Lydia had finally turned around, had barely got hold of the photograph, when the nursing aide bolted out of the room as if pursued by malevolent spirits. An acrid taste rose from the pit of Lydia's stomach. She stared at her stillborn son's colour image, a silent protest lodged in the back of her throat.

He's dead. Still dead. It will never change. He'll always be dead!

They gave her a painkiller and it soon made her drowsy again. She fell into a morning slumber, dreaming of a neighbour they'd had when she was a child, still sleeping in one room with her two siblings, on a lambswool mattress. She would have been eight or nine when their neighbour lost her first child.

"Why was Stamatoula taken to the hospital, Mama?"

"Women's problems."

That was all her mother would say on that balmy Independence Day, wearing the shuttered expression she wore whenever these two words were uttered. Lydia had been hearing them as far back as she could remember, had learned to watch and listen, without asking a lot of intrusive questions. But that spring day she felt too muddled to keep quiet.

"What happened?" she insisted.

There had been whispered exchanges among the neighbourhood's women, and some of her own playmates. Lydia knew that Stamatoula had been pregnant, but babies, in her limited experience, did not seem to belong in the same obscure realm as Women's Problems. She watched her mother peel potatoes that morning, wiping tears with the corner of her apron.

"What happened to the baby, Mama?"

"It became an angel." Lydia's mother sighed. "Why are you staring at me like that? One of God's little angels."

Thereafter, babies, too, had a place in the multiple chambers of Women's Problems. By the time she reached puberty, Lydia had come to feel that the secret domain was as vast as it was murky.

The signposts, however, must have gradually become familiar. By the time she began menstruating—at fourteen, very late compared to her new Canadian friends—she knew that hereafter the grounds would no longer be off-limits to her. She was, she understood with trepidation, about to be initiated into its boundless mysteries.

The move to Canada had marked the beginning of some sort of internal havoc. Lydia—a hitherto cheerful child—was suddenly crying on a regular basis and would do so throughout adolescence, sometimes for no apparent reason. Her mother kept wagging her head, saying it was all about being uprooted from their beloved homeland. But that long Labour Day weekend, on her newly stained Canadian mattress, Lydia had known why she was crying.

She was now a woman.

18

The moment John opened the front door, their two cats leapt from the hallway rug and came rushing at him with indignant cries. Lydia usually fed them when she rose at seven. In his rush to leave the house yesterday, he had forgotten to add extra food in the cats' bowl. Though it was now only 8:30 in the morning, they circled him as he shucked off his shoes, their tails in the air, whining.

John picked up the mail, desperate for coffee. Claire had been in deep sleep when he left her condo. He had an office appointment at ten and two consultations in the afternoon.

"W-a-i-t!" he snapped at the cats. Fucking beasts, he thought. Won't even let you relieve yourself. "Go away! Scram!"

But the cats, as if spurred by his flaring temper, howled more insistently than ever. Sappho lunged at him, digging her claws through the bottom of his pants.

"Fuck off!" John shook his leg free, heading for the kitchen. And then he caught sight of the living room. "Oh Jesus Christ!"

Magazines and books were strewn all over the floor, one of his pipes lay by the fireplace, a small flower pot with a blooming orchid had been overturned. No serious damage, he noted, relieved. In his irritation, though, he came close to kicking one of the cats when she tried to have another go at his leg.

Sappho was a fat Persian, with blue eyes and a long silver coat. Slow and placid, she was nonetheless the first to protest whenever her needs were not promptly satisfied. A diva. She had a slightly croaky voice that grated on John's nerves even at the best of times. Somehow, Lydia did not seem to mind. He suspected she liked the sense of being needed, of placating hunger, treating rashes, scratches. The most maternal woman he'd ever known.

A sudden wave of guilt washed over his heart. Had he, all these years, been the husband a woman like her deserved? Had he even been sufficiently supportive during his recent hospital visits? How cruel of the God his mother so fervently believed in to deprive a woman like Lydia of the child she longed for, and so clearly deserved.

His head still aching, John poured dry Purina into the plastic dishes set on a rubber mat in the butler's pantry. The cats, however, only sniffed the pellets and quickly resumed whining.

Only then did John remember Lydia saying that, perversely, they ate dry food only when they were not really hungry. No choice but to quickly give them what they wanted if he was to have any peace this morning. But first he must attend to his own urgent needs. He made a dash for the powder room.

But here, too, there was evidence of feline rage. The wastebasket was overturned, the guest towels lay in a heap on the floor tiles. Swearing under his breath, he relieved himself, then hastened to open a can of Friskies. He then plugged in the kettle and sat down to sort out the mail.

There was a Greek postcard of a famous cliff-top church, sent by Lydia's vacationing brother and sister-in-law. There was also a Mexican card from his own sister. He would take the cards to the hospital. Lydia will be pleased to know that Helen would be back by the end of this week.

But why were the cats pestering him again?

He spun and glared at them, heat rising behind his eyes. He could not remember the last time he had felt so thoroughly vexed.

"What now?!" he bellowed. "I fed you, didn't I? What the fuck do you want from me?"

The kettle began to whistle and he went about making a fresh pot of coffee. He finally opened a second can of Friskies because, for some reason, the cats seemed exceptionally hungry today.

It did not stop their howling.

And then, all at once, he perceived the problem. He had, on arriving home, absent-mindedly shut the door to the closet that held the cats' litter box (he was always shutting open doors after Lydia). The cats had kept going in that direction but he had been too distracted to respond to their frantic signals.

It was too late now.

At precisely the moment he understood the problem, Sappho was crouching a few steps away, daintily relieving herself on the kitchen floor. He thanked his stars that it was the tiled kitchen floor and not one of their Persian rugs.

He dropped the mail on the kitchen table and blotted up the puddle with paper towels. He squirted some soap and mopped up the spot, then sprayed it with disinfectant. He then poured himself a fresh cup of coffee.

It was by now nine-thirty and the weather looked like it might finally be clearing. Through the open window, he could hear their neighbour, Mrs. Farquhar, chatting up a friendly postman, who had stopped to pet her black, bushy-tailed cat.

The neighbour was a recently widowed woman in her early seventies. It was Lydia who had got her the kitten when Mr. Farquhar had passed away last fall, and the poor woman could never stop expressing her gratitude. She must, John supposed, be lonely after some fifty years of marriage, for she seemed reluctant to let the postman go. They chatted on the stoop for a few minutes, then the postman wished Mrs. Farquhar a good day, adjusted the strap on his canvas mailbag, and walked on, whistling.

John closed his eyes and sat for a while in the suddenly silent kitchen, startled when Sappho leapt onto his knees and settled herself, purring, in his lap, rubbing her head against his abdomen. John absently stroked the cat's head, as if his fingers had a will of their own. Becoming aware of what he was doing, he impulsively gathered the cat in his arms and cuddled her closely against his chest, murmuring his apologies.

Sappho went on purring. John surprised himself again, weeping into the cat's abundant fur like a disconsolate child.

19

Her husband arrived sometime before noon, bringing her favourite chocolates as well as the pyjamas she had requested. He was now ensconced in the visitor's chair, doing his best to talk her out of something she insisted must be done as soon as possible. She wanted their baby's things given away before she returned home—everything in the nursery: crib, toys, clothes. Every single thing! If necessary, she would stay with her mother for a few days until it was all gone.

The request elicited one of John's heaviest sighs. He went on trying to reason with her—she might get pregnant again one of these days. He kept stroking her hand as he said this, finger after finger.

"You'll feel much better once you're home," he added. "I was thinking of taking at least a month off this winter. We could go to Bora Bora or the Seychelles...just name the place and I'll make it happen."

"Oh!" she flashed at him. "Do you think there are no babies outside this hospital?" She had raised her head and was staring at him with glittering hostility. "Most people have children," she said. "That's all they talk about half the time. Anywhere you go!"

He gazed at her for a prolonged moment. "I know it must seem that way right now," he told her at length. "But you'll be all right in a month or two, then—"

"A month or two!" She jerked up, her eyes stinging. "You really don't understand, do you? You can't imagine what it's like. Only a woman can...someone who's been through it!"

She breathed deeply, her hand on her distended breasts. "I'll never be all right again. Never!" The word echoed in the small room, silent but for the rain throbbing at the windows. "I haven't really been all right since the miscarriage—maybe since the abortion, even. Oh," she trailed off. "Don't look at me like that! Please!"

He was gazing at her with skeptical eyes, like a stern parent doing his best to believe a beloved child's fib.

"Lydia," he finally said. "Don't do this to yourself, I beg you! You had the abortion thirteen years ago." The last statement was made calmly, a little incredulously. Lydia stared at him for a moment: his slate-grey eyes that gave nothing away, his neatly arched eyebrows. At last, her simmering anger came fizzing to the surface.

"It may have been thirteen years ago, but I know... we both know the whole thing's your fault!" She looked him straight in the eye, the corners of her mouth twitching, seeing him shrink back, as if he had been struck.

He said, "My fault? What do you mean?" His eyes had a shocked, slightly wounded look. "How is it my fault?"

At this, Lydia raised her hands and dropped her face into them. "It's impossible to talk to you!" she said in a hopeless voice. "You pretend, you—who do you think you're talking to, a perfect stranger?"

She lowered her hands. She was burning, burning with unfamiliar flames: fury and grief and simmering resentment. John opened his mouth, as if to protest, but got to his feet instead and began to pace alongside her bed.

He said, "Lydia—" then stopped, looking down at her with his fine eyebrows knitted. "I know you're very upset, but—"

"Upset?!" she cut in savagely. "I am devastated, John! Whereas you...you didn't even want the baby in the first place." She stared at him bitterly, groping for a tissue. "What, you thought I didn't know?"

"Lydia!" For the first time John seemed on the verge of losing his equanimity. He returned to the visitor's chair, looking dumbfounded. "What is this?

What has gotten into you?" He regarded her with an expression of dazed reproach. "Why should I not want my own child?" He took out his pipe from sheer habit, but quickly put it away again. "Talk to me," he said. "Please."

"I don't know." Lydia rolled onto her back with a laboured sigh. Her eyes were searching the ceiling. "I don't know," she repeated. She stopped and blew her nose. "I sometimes think your mother's hoping you might divorce me if we don't have children," she said, feeling her eyelid twitch. She knew his parents had disapproved of his marrying her, a Greek villager's daughter. "I think…I feel…"

He would not let her finish. "I'm sorry, my dear," he said, "but your feminine intuition has let you down this time." He shifted his weight, looking at her severely. "Actually, my mother would like nothing better than to have a grandchild."

"A grandchild, yes! But not mine, not Lydia Dimou's!" Though her voice quivered, there was no stopping now. "You should've seen her last week when she came to see me. I could read it so plainly." She began to cry.

"But read what, for God's sake? What did she say?" John's voice grew thin with exasperation. When Lydia would not answer, he threw his head back and closed his eyes, breathing through his mouth. His wife went on weeping.

"Lydia, listen to me—Lydia! You've been through the mill, darling," John said, his hand flying to his forehead. "And your...your..." He stopped himself, shaking his head. "Good God, I had no idea...I hardly know what to say right now!"

Lydia glanced up, registering the pain shadowing his eyes. He looked as helpless as a child, at once dazed and wounded. There was something about him that, on occasion, made her see her husband as he must have been as a boy: a reserved, vulnerable child, teased for his skinny torso, his lack of interest in sports.

All at once, remorse flooded her heart. She inched herself to an upright position. "I'm sorry, John."

He raised his hand and fitfully passed it over his face. "I had no idea," he said yet again. "I wish you'd talked to me."

"I'm sorry," she repeated lamely. "I think I am losing my mind."

"You're not...believe me, you're not," he repeated. "Your hormones are..."

Lydia looked about to protest but there was a knock on the door. A kitchen aide entered, wearing a hairnet, carrying a lunch tray. She glanced from John to Lydia, smiled shyly, and was leaving the room when John's pager buzzed.

"I'd better go now," he said, having checked the number. "I have to look in on a patient." He had operated on the man's lungs last Thursday; earlier this morning, about to be discharged, the patient suddenly began to have trouble breathing. Was there to be no end to his problems this week?

John bent over and kissed Lydia's cheek, lingering for another moment. "Please try to be positive, darling," he said. He took her hand in his. "Just give it time," he added, gazing into her face. "Everything's going to be okay in time."

"Oh." Lydia sighed, her eyes brimming. "If only I could believe that!"

"Believe it," said John.

20

John was about to enter the hospital cafeteria when he ran into Claire. Like him, she was on her way to a late lunch.

"Ah, just the man I was looking for!" She unsnapped her handbag and pulled out a pair of black leather gloves. "You forgot these this morning."

"Oh, thank you! I've been looking for them." John pocketed the gloves, glancing about nervously. "I can't believe what's happening to me," he said. "I've become so fucking absent-minded!"

Claire gave him a complicated look, at once sympathetic and reproachful. "Don't be so hard on yourself," she said. "This too shall pass."

The entrance to the cafeteria—the entire hospital lobby—reeked of baked fish. John consulted his watch, then half-turned toward the main entrance. "Look," he said, "the sun seems to be coming out. Are you pressed for time?" He paused to greet a passing colleague. "There's a new Thai restaurant on the corner. It's casual, but bound to be a cut above hospital haddock." He achieved something resembling a smile. "What do you say?"

She hesitated for the briefest moment. He could see her scanning his face, taking in his haggard features.

"Oh, why not?" she finally said. She offered one of her dazzling smiles, but John had not failed to take note of the flicker of doubt.

It occurred to him that he was making excessive demands on Claire, he would not blame her if she'd had enough of his anguished ramblings. He wished it had been possible to hire her professional services. He could have paid her and not have to feel he was taking advantage of their liaison. The relationship, in any case, would be over soon. He was sure about that, feeling doubly guilty. Right now, they were just two colleagues about to enjoy a casual lunch. He would do his best to keep his personal problems to himself. He would not so much as mention his visit with Lydia.

They crossed the lobby, then made their way toward the restaurant on the corner of Côte-des-Neiges. Above them, the sun kept peeping between drifting clouds, like a promissory note.

The restaurant was nearly empty and they settled themselves in the back, by one of the windows. Claire took off her blazer and draped it over the chair. She had, John observed, trimmed her eyebrows and cut her bangs, looking more alluring than ever. She had on a greyish-green top matching her eyes.

"This is nice," she said, glancing about appraisingly. "How long has the restaurant been here?"

"I'm not sure. Two or three months, I think."

John put on his reading glasses and opened the menu. "As I said: an improvement over desiccated fish."

They opted for the Lunch Specials. Claire ordered lemongrass soup, John choosing spicy chicken soup with rice noodles. He still had very little appetite, but both his mother and Lydia had been nagging him to make sure he did not skip meals.

John checked his pager and put it away in his pocket. Having resolved to steer clear of personal concerns, he did his best to show interest in Claire's life for a change. He tried to get her to talk about the book she was working on, but she seemed a little evasive. Early on in their relationship, when he first asked her about the novel, she had quoted Fellini, who was on record stating that any movie he happened to discuss never saw the light of day.

"Are you superstitious?" he asked now.

"Yes, a little, but...it's just not going very well right now. I've decided to take a break." She gave him a bright, quirky smile. "You're just the excuse I needed."

"Oh, is that right? I hope I haven't given you a bigger excuse than you'd bargained for," said John, smiling at her lamely.

Claire made a dismissive gesture. She was having trouble with one of her fictional characters, was not sure she understood a certain kind of man as well as she needed to, she confided. Her restless gaze wandered toward a couple seated at the next table, chatting away in French. She watched them for a moment, then turned back to John, steering the conversation toward a bit of hospital gossip.

It was all about a recently widowed cardiologist, an observant Jew who was about to marry a much younger French-Canadian woman he had met through personal ads. The woman was a chef at a fine Montreal restaurant but was reportedly learning to prepare traditional Jewish dishes. The cardiologist liked to boast about her culinary skills. Her gefilte fish was every bit as good as his mother's, he was heard to say to anyone who would listen.

John managed a chuckle. "My father used to say the same thing about my mother's stuffed eggplants. It's still his favourite dish to this day."

"Hm. I don't think I've ever had stuffed eggplants," said Claire, taking a sip of water. "My mother's idea of a nutritious dinner was canned asparagus soup with a bit of cheese, and beans on toast. I suppose your mother spent her days making homemade pasta and rolling vine leaves?"

"Yes, indeed." John smiled. "I don't think you'd find a Greek mother who would serve canned soup to her family."

"Really? Even in this day and age?" said Claire. "Don't Greek-Canadian mothers work?"

"Some do," said John. "They still wouldn't serve canned soup, I don't think."

"Hm," said Claire. The waiter had just arrived with their main dishes. They had both ordered shrimps in spicy coconut sauce. It came with white rice and a bit of salad.

"Speaking of mothers," said Claire once the waiter had gone, "I've been mulling over something you said the other day.

"Oh?" said John. "About my mother?"

"Not just your mother. I've been thinking—not for the first time, mind you—that women themselves can be largely responsible for the way so many men treat their wives." She paused, taking a big swallow of water. The dish was a little too spicy for her, she managed to let out.

John dabbed at his mouth with a napkin. "I know some feminists who would crucify you for what you just said."

"I know," said Claire, "I know! But virtually every woman I've ever met said that her brothers got preferential treatment from their mother—especially in traditional families. It's not the mother's fault, but she reinforces the system—without even realizing how unfair it is."

John wiped his mouth. "My sister would certainly agree with that," he said.

"Oh, I expect she would," Claire answered. "She might even agree that this is why men all over the world are the way they are. You all want to be in charge, to make all the big decisions, but also—" She swallowed, looking straight into John's eyes. "To have someone who'll go on mothering you for the rest of your life."

John pondered this for a moment. He consulted his watch, then signalled the waiter for coffee. "And you think that's my problem too, do you?"

"I think that very few men can cope with marital equality."

"Oh, well." John sighed, feeling vaguely miffed. "And here I was, thinking I should stop all my navel-gazing. I thought—" He pushed his plate aside and leaned back in his chair. The waiter was coming up, bearing two cups of coffee.

"You thought—?"

"Never mind," said John. He reached for a napkin.

"How about dessert?" the waiter inquired.

"Not for me, thank you," Claire said, fiddling with an earring. "You?" she asked John.

"No, thanks." He groped for his wallet. He had a three-thirty appointment and had to be getting back. He looked out the window. The sky, which had briefly appeared to be clearing up, was clouding over again. "Shall we go?"

"Yes," she said, turning to get her blazer. She was going back to the hospital; he would walk down one block to his private office. They waited for the light to change. They were about to say goodbye, but Claire paused to search his face.

"I'm worried about you," she said, frowning. "Feel free to drop in again if you can't stand being alone, you hear?"

"Oh, I don't know. I might," said John. He turned to leave.

"Take care of yourself," said Claire.

"You too." John managed a smile, then said goodbye and headed downhill, checking his pager as he walked toward the medical building housing his office. There had been two calls, one from his mother, the other from his mother-in-law.

He let out a sigh. The thought of having to face both women again made fresh despair rise in his throat. Claire was apparently worried that he might crack up, and perhaps rightly so. The lunch had done nothing to improve his mood. The elevator was crowded and, for a moment, he felt the threat of claustrophobia.

Briskly, he stepped off the elevator and trudged down the long, neon-lit corridor. Only the sight of his own office door somewhat restored his inner equilibrium. He had moved into this office only two months earlier and had been happy with his choice. His name was freshly painted on the frosted glass; he could hear the phone ringing as he opened the door. In the reception area, a middle-aged couple sat awaiting his arrival, looking anxious and rather deferential. Dianne, his secretary, reached for the ringing telephone, but not before bestowing on him a warm, welcoming smile.

"Dr. Gabriel's office."

21

Lydia had been working at the Montreal General Hospital, secretary to Dr. Matthew Harding, the Surgeon-in-Chief, when she first met Dr. John Gabriel.

He was a surgical resident at the time, a tall young man with thick, dark hair and a lean, intense face vaguely reminiscent of the young Abraham Lincoln. He, too, was Greek, but his was a prosperous family. His father was a wine importer, Lydia's dad a former stonemason. Phevos Dimou had come to Canada hoping to get rich, but had found only factory work, forcing his wife to take in other women's sewing.

Having chatted a few times in Dr. Harding's office, Lydia and John began to meet secretly—usually in the residents' quarters—and quietly went about having an abortion before the year was out.

Secrecy suited them both: Lydia because her father would not have permitted dating, and John, she suspected, because he was a little embarrassed by their relations. She could acknowledge this to herself now that she had a university degree, drove a car, and shopped at Ogilvy and Holt Renfrew, if only during special sales.

She was not the naive girl she had been when they started dating but could never quite shake off the knowledge that theirs was what used to be called a "shotgun marriage."

She had come across the expression years ago in some old novel she had picked up at a neighbourhood garage sale. Somehow, despite all precautions, she had become pregnant a second time. They had by then been dating for over two years; John was close to completing his training, had managed to talk Lydia into taking a couple of university courses.

And so they finally married, keeping the pregnancy to themselves for now. How happy she had been, learning that her in-laws had generously offered a Greek honeymoon as a wedding present! Would they have done so had they known that their son's bride was already expecting a child?

A honeymoon, but not very sweet.

They started by touring the Peloponnese, where John's family originated, then travelled by sea to Lesbos. They had been forced to take the slow ferry boat from Piraeus: fourteen hours on the third-class deck because domestic flights were booked up and all the cabins had long since been reserved.

Nobody had thought to tell them about making domestic arrangements in what both John and Lydia had assumed would be a quiet off-season. Neither the Canadian travel agent nor John's parents, and certainly not his Greek relatives in Sparta.

But John became uncharacteristically grumpy during the sea passage, as if it had somehow been Lydia's fault; as if she had withheld the travel information for the express purpose of forcing him to spend a long night on a crowded deck, surrounded by peasants eating bread with olives, and unshaven soldiers on furlough. As if this was the way *she* preferred to travel, wearing her beautiful new dress and light summer blazer, surrounded by the smell of ripe cheese and canned sardines.

It had not been her fault, but the truth was she had not especially minded. Was that why she had seen his irritability as unvoiced accusation?

He had been distracted in Sparta, too, but she could not find it in her heart to blame him then. He had just met a young cousin who was mute from childhood meningitis and, more distressingly, his maternal uncle, who had pancreatic cancer and for whom nothing could be done.

And then she lost her ring. Washing her hands in the ferry boat's squalid bathroom, she saw it disappear down the open drain. Her new, shiny, gold wedding ring.

"But how?" John demanded, frowning at the sign on the toilet door—a woman leading a small pink poodle—through which he had been urgently summoned. "How does anyone lose a brand new ring down the drain?" He stood cracking his knuckles, squinting into the gaping black hole.

"Well," she said, "it's just a bit big, you know, my hands were full of soap."

It had not occurred to her to say, as she might have now, that a new ring is not necessarily harder to lose than a tarnished one. He'd looked stern and humourless in that public bathroom, casting about for something with which he might try to retrieve the ring.

"We'd better get help," he finally said.

Eventually, a plumber was found and tools were fetched and, along with rotting hair and lipstick and a yellowing contact lens, the wedding ring was at last retrieved, shining brightly in the plumber's bucket. But by then Lydia had resigned herself to both loss and her own carelessness. On the deck, the soldiers sang. The moon shed its pale light on the sleeping peasants. His child was in her womb. She listened to the Greek love songs, the churning waves; the possibility, much too early, of her baby's movements. What was he thinking?

She didn't ask. She chose not to tell him about her spotted pants during their honeymoon, or even after they were back home in Montreal. She would not have been able to explain it then, but, after all these years, alone in her hospital room, could finally do so. Of course, she could not tell him about the sudden spotting, fearing his inner reaction even more than the possibility of losing her baby.

It was all for nothing. I married you for nothing.

22

A fruit basket in one hand, a newspaper under his arm, John Gabriel stepped out of St. Margaret's elevator and nearly collided with a former patient. They both hastened to step aside, muttering apologies.

"Dr. Gabriel! Don't you remember me?" The sun-bronzed man extended a hand, then grinned, flushing a little: he had forced his former doctor to put his basket down on the floor.

"Oh, hello! Yes, of course." John shook his ex-patient's hand. "I'm bad with names though. You are—"

"Frank Petersen, I was—"

"Oh, yes, I remember you." A round, good-natured face, a wrestler's physique. "How are you doing?" Petersen was fumbling in his trench-coat pocket. He would be in his mid-30s now.

"Fine, fine, couldn't be better." The erstwhile patient chuckled, holding out a box of Dutch cigars. "My wife just gave birth." His strong, white teeth glinted with satisfaction.

"Well! Congratulations!" John did his best to inject some warmth into his smile. "I'm pleased to hear that. Boy or girl?"

"Boy!" Frank Petersen said. And John thought: ah, the pride on that jock's face. "Eight pounds ten ounces. Pretty good, eh?"

Again, John offered his congratulations. He then glanced down the hall, hoping to make his intentions clear.

"Would you like to see him, he's—"

"Well—" John made a show of consulting his watch. "I'm sorry, I'm...late as it is." He had caught himself just in time; had all but said he was on his way to visit his wife. "Give my regards to Mrs. Petersen." They shook hands once more. "Good luck with the youngster."

John bent down to retrieve the fruit basket.

He remembered the insurance salesman all right. Remembered all of them; every man and woman he had ever faced with the unnerving C word. Though patients' names often eluded him, the faces remained with him. Sometimes he dreamed about them, huddled together behind a wire fence like concentration camp inmates.

He had over the years learned how to deal with his distressed patients, had learned to give hope, to face relatives and lovers, yet he could never quite get rid of his festering guilt. For being the bearer of bad news? For being himself a relatively young, healthy man?

He really couldn't say. He knew only one thing: the more content he felt on any given day, the more heavily the weight of his own failures fell upon his shoulders. He felt that his patients' relatives held him, if not exactly responsible for the disease, then for not being able to cure it.

People were not always rational when it came to cancer. His own uncle, dying in Sparta the summer he and Lydia were visiting, had pounced on their unexpected visit as if God himself had sent him a personal saviour. His nephew, he told everyone, a Canadian-trained surgeon! Of course he would get better. John was bound to know something the doctors in Sparta didn't. The poor man, dying of pancreatic cancer, actually got out of bed after their arrival and walked around for the first time in weeks.

This was perhaps what had spoiled John's honeymoon for him. How was a man to enjoy himself, hike in the countryside, swim in the sea, when he lacked the power to say Yes to the question in a dying man's eyes?

Yes, he had been moody, with his relatives as well as with Lydia. He was by nature inclined to slide into grim silence when faced with expectations he could not fulfill. And there were his mother's sisters, his cousins, his cousins' children—all, even the youngest of them, looking up at him with their supplicant eyes, like Christ's disciples in medieval paintings.

And yet, he had promised nothing, had claimed no special powers. What right did they have to make him feel it was somehow his fault? Because, yes, he'd finally had to tell them, make them accept the obvious: a surgeon, Canadian born and trained, he was still just a man. He could not stay with them, as they had begged him to, did not possess talismanic powers. But they had held onto him, literally clutched onto his hands, his sleeves, sure that death would come as soon as he had left them.

Which, sadly, it did. The news reached them on Lesbos, via his mother, with Lydia's superstitious relatives hovering about obsequiously, as if to lose favour might cost them their lives as well. He couldn't wait to get away from them, though in time he would come to understand that superstition was just a sad expression of human impotence before the randomness of fate.

Now, heading toward Lydia's room, John thought of Frank Petersen, whose cancerous testicle he had detected by mere chance (Petersen had come to him for a cyst), hoping that the biopsy would disprove his tentative diagnosis. Sadly, it hadn't. Petersen was sent to a urologist; John had not been the one to excise the diseased testicle. All the same, he had felt ill at ease, running just now into the beaming father, startled and dismayed by his own resentment.

He paused and composed himself. He knocked on Lydia's door.

23

"Marriage is one thing I seem to have no talent for," John's sister had been heard to say on more than one occasion.

Helen was close to her brother, but closer still to Lydia. She was the older, wiser, sister Lydia had always wanted: well-travelled, independent, outspoken to a fault. Unlike her brother or for that matter Lydia, Helen was blithely forthright with her friends. She had occasionally embarrassed Lydia with questions like, "How's your sex life?" or "Were you a virgin when you married my brother?"

She was a tall, animated woman with restless gestures and unpredictable habits. She often dressed eccentrically, her clothes held together with safety pins and colourful belts. She could not be bothered to go on shopping sprees, or stand before the mirror long enough to see what went with what.

Unlike her brother, Helen wore whatever came her way—blue jeans from The Gap, colourful shawls acquired at Turkish bazaars, Afghani socks, sexy French shoes. She dazzled Lydia with her flair, her verve, her adventures as a CBC correspondent. She did not, Lydia felt, belong in the Gabriel family. She belonged in a Leonard Cohen song, their own intrepid Suzanne.

Helen for her part claimed to like nothing better than to be invited for dinner at her brother's house. Every now and then, she'd confessed to Lydia, she felt like a freak, gazing longingly at the tidy interiors of other people's homes.

"The frilly curtains, the flowerpots on the windowsills." There were times when, passing through some foreign town, she would find herself swept by a wave of longing.

"Longing for what, exactly?" Lydia could not help asking.

"For...exactly what you've got here," said Helen with a sweeping gesture. There were evenings when she would have gladly traded places with anyone reading a book or watching TV in their own quiet den.

Lydia placed a coffee cup before Helen. "Would you like to trade places with me—right here, right now?"

"Of course not," said Helen. "That would be incest!" And they laughed together, the coffee spilling into their saucers. Helen took a napkin and placed it under her cup. "The thing is," she said, "your life's so incredibly orderly. It's so fucking serene."

"Oh, it only seems like that from the outside," Lydia said lightly. She could not bear the thought of anyone envying her, least of all dear Helen.

But all that had taken place long ago. Right now, Lydia was propped up in her hospital bed, re-reading the card John had brought, along with one sent by her own brother in mid-August, but delivered several days after Andreas and his family had returned from their annual trip to Greece. Helen's postcard was of the sort sold in museum gift shops all over the world. A small reproduction of a painting by a Mexican artist Lydia had never heard of. *Still Life with a Dog.*

"I picked it up," Helen wrote in her tiny script, *"because it made me think of your dining room. The bowl of fruit, the flowers, the pretty decanter (I thought of the great bottle of Boutari we polished off on my last visit). Do you like it? It has not only the colours but the atmosphere of your home, Lydia. The sense of beauty, order, tranquility. As if the precise spot for the decanter were marked on the table; as if there were always 3 apples, 2 pears, 1 orange, and a bunch of red grapes placed just so.*

But the thing that interested me most of all was the dog in the corner (not a cat!); the way it sits there, eyeing that bowl of fruit. It looks so obedient, doesn't it? And the fruit looks so perfect, it seems almost staged! I keep feeling the dog's about to pounce on that lovely bowl and send the fruit rolling off. Not that dogs like fruit but that's what this dog's eyes seem to be saying to me. Maybe I just wish it would do that. Put some life into this still life! That's all for now. No more space for my flights of fancy. I'll be back after Labour Day. Looking forward to meeting my nephew! Love and kisses, Helen.

24

"Please don't cry, darling," John said, sounding fatuous even to his own ears.

He had come into his wife's hospital room and found her slumped against the white pillows, her face a weeping mask. She avoided meeting his gaze but lay with her eyes fixated on the ceiling, silent tears rolling down her face.

"I've brought you some nice fruit," he said lamely.

He lowered himself onto the edge of the bed and saw her wince as she shifted her bulk a little. Only then did he notice his son's photograph, resting on one of the bedside tables. The setting sun filled the room with its fickle autumnal light. "Are you in pain? Would you like me to get the nurse?"

"Yes," she said. "Please."

She kept her eyes averted as she spoke, her face grey as dishwater. The window had been left open, but the fresh air only seemed to sharpen the mingling odours of hospital food, disinfectant, sweat. She wanted an analgesic, so he went to the nursing station and returned with a nurse bearing a tiny pill cup. He went to use the toilet, then came out to find the nurse gone and Lydia lying motionless as a mummy, her eyes shut.

"I'm here," he said softly, sitting down to stroke her bare arm. What was there to say? There were things he had wanted to tell her but was not sure about voicing them now. His wife had become as unpredictable as a stranger. She had picked up the photograph and was staring at it with brimming eyes.

"It could've been much worse, you know," John said, speaking very gently. "He might have been born disabled or chronically ill or—"

"But he wasn't!" she cut in with feeling. "He was perfect—perfect!" She regarded him for a moment with blurred eyes in which, heavy-hearted, he gradually perceived nothing but dying hope. She turned and blew her nose, dabbing at her blotched face with a crumpled tissue. There was a tired feeling in his chest, a sense of spreading futility. He watched her lips tighten

"I've been thinking, you know?" she finally said. "I think it was probably something the doctors or nurses did. Something went wrong somewhere." She gave him a long, anguished stare, visibly struggling with her own emotions. "Why else would Dr. Minnaar look so...furtive?" she demanded. And then her face crumpled up. She began to weep more noisily, talking through her sobs.

"They still don't know why it happened. The baby was born alive—he was born alive!" The statement ended in a sort of wail. Convulsively, Lydia raised her hands and sobbed for a long moment while John sat slumped beside her, stroking her wild curls.

Though he had seen the obstetrician only briefly on Monday, it was in him to explain what he surely understood better than most husbands: the devastating awareness of one's own professional failure; the pain and embarrassment and guilt that came at such moments, notwithstanding the knowledge of one's best efforts. And yes, the compulsion to run off and hide, which was, he supposed, what Lydia had seen in Thomas Minnaar's eyes.

John was still groping for words with which to comfort his wife when she raised her gaze and said: "We can have an official inquest, can't we? Maybe even sue him?"

"Lydia." John went on stroking her hair though his hand was shaky. "I'm sure Minnaar...I'm sure they all did what they could, believe me. I am certain they did." His eyes gazed into hers with wordless sympathy. He was silent for a long moment. "It was most likely a lack of oxygen," he finally said, then sighed: he had not meant it to sound so clinical. "That's what it is most often."

"But why?" she insisted. "Why, when he was so perfect?"

John sighed again, looking at her with commiserating eyes.

Why.

He wished he could answer her; he sincerely did. Something stirred in his chest. He was perspiring heavily and his knees began to feel rubbery. Yes, he wished he could give her more than medical facts—all feeble speculation in any case—which he nonetheless ventured when she suddenly turned away from him and hid her face, shaking with unleashed grief.

"Lydia, Lydia," he said, a wave of crushing helplessness washing over him. "Lydia, listen to me. Please, darling."

God, what could he do to help her? He closed his eyes for a moment and let out another heavy sigh. There was a stale taste in his mouth. Would she ever recover from this? he wondered grimly. Or would this crushing grief drive her to the edge of madness?

John was at a loss for comforting words, but his heart was filled with infinite sorrow, watching his wife weep in that crisp white bed while dusk descended, sweeping the room with shadows. He went on stroking her arm, thinking: *let her cry...she needs to grieve right now...as long as it takes.*

After a while, though, he could not help himself. He said, "You're still young, Lydia, you're only thirty-three—"

She jerked herself upright. "Oh—!" she cried, seeming to choke on the utterance. There was a bitter, accusing light in her eyes as she went on coughing, sniffling—struggling, he thought, to express some unassailable truth.

But then, as if overcome by unbearable weariness, her eyes seemed to grow dark and hollow. She fell back with a moan and resumed crying more quietly while, out in the corridor, the P.A. system announced visiting hours over, for everyone except new fathers.

John planted a tender kiss on Lydia's forehead, then reached out and turned on the overheard light.

His wife's crying had become listless, barely audible. He felt as if the two of them had been locked up in some isolated cell, surrounded by voices, laughter—an endless traffic of patients, relatives, nurses. Their exchanges came to him in oddly remote snatches, as if he were separated from them not by a single unlocked door but some impenetrable brick wall that had him trapped, doomed to spend the rest of his days with his despairing wife. She was still quietly weeping, seemingly oblivious to his earnest desire to comfort and solace.

He would have to stay, father though he wasn't, and suffer what to him was perhaps the greatest affliction of all: the knowledge of his own impotence. There was nothing he could do right now but somehow convey his love and do his best to fulfill his wife's requests, whatever they might be.

And so he remained seated beside her, taut and silent, aware only of distant corridor sounds, his own physical discomfort, Lydia's endless tears.

But, after a while, those too seemed to be losing their momentum. She had asked for more water and was drinking it when a nurse came back to check her vitals and change her soaked pad.

John stepped out of the room, letting a young orderly pass, pushing an enormous cart laden with piles of medical supplies. An ambulance went by with its siren blaring. And then Lydia's voice reached him, muffled, through the closed door.

"I can't go home," he heard her say to the nurse. "I want to go home but I just can't. I think we may have jinxed ourselves, you know, getting all that baby stuff while I was still pregnant."

"Oh no," the nurse hastened to put in. "I'm sure that's not true. You don't really believe that, do you?"

"No...but I can't help it," said Lydia's voice. She sounded, once more, on the verge of tears.

"You mustn't," said the nurse. "You mustn't think like that, dear."

John knocked on the door and re-entered the room. The nurse seemed to be done. She was leaning over Lydia, stroking her mass of curls. Overcome by an intensely protective impulse, John rushed to his wife's bedside.

"I'm back," he said quietly. "I'm back, my dear."

THURSDAY
September 5, 1991

25

There were two almond trees in their Greek village garden, one of which bore fruit every single year while the other never did. The garden was large and shady, fragrant with lilac and wisteria blossoms. Lydia's earliest memories were of herself as a toddler, stumbling on the cobblestones, peering into the chicken coop, saying *ko-ko-ko*. A mysterious garden, vibrant with bees and robins and purring turtle doves.

And, of course, children. Lydia, the eldest, was in charge of her brother and sister, but there were often young cousins or neighbours around, and distant relatives from nearby villages. In Lydia's recollections, there were always children of all ages, chasing each other around the ancient fig tree, playing hide-and-seek.

Relatives usually came during the holidays: Easter and Christmas and Holy Cross Day. At Christmas they sat indoors around the old wood stove, but at Easter, except once or twice when it happened to rain, they gathered outside to roast the traditional lamb. The almonds were not yet ripe at that time of year but the children liked to eat them raw, green and crunchy and a little sour. *Tsaghala*.

By mid-August, when they celebrated the Day of the Assumption, the figs had ripened, bursting with seed and syrup. They ate some of the figs, then made preserves and compotes, but still there were basketfuls of them. The fruit was left out in the sun to dry, along with the egg noodles they had rolled all summer.

In mid-September, when Holy Cross Day came, the almonds finally ripened and were left out in the sun as well. Lydia was expected to help with all these domestic chores. When the almonds dried out, she would sit on the garden steps and split them open with a large stone, shell them, and sometimes grind them with a mortar and pestle, to be used in cakes and cookies.

One year, there was an exceptionally abundant crop. Lydia recalled that autumn vividly because that was the fall her father left them and flew, for the first time, to Athens, and then to Canada. She was ten years old. On the last Sunday before his departure, the house was packed with neighbours and relatives, arriving all day to offer their final greetings.

It was early October, a mild, sunny day marred by a touch of sadness. Phevos Dimou was leaving the island of his birth! Lydia could not imagine their family life without her father. She talked little throughout the festivities. Now and then she saw her mother dab at her eyes with a handkerchief.

But soon they were all laughing in the garden, eating almond macaroons and drinking coffee or ouzo, praising what there was to praise: the enormous catch of tuna that week. And the olive crop, which promised to be plentiful if the rains came as expected. And, of course, the robust children, two of whom had just been baptized that summer. It had been a good, fecund year. Praise be to the Lord for all these blessings.

Lydia, though, was old enough to know that they all had their private sorrows: a shortage of money, an ailing child or parent. The women sighed while their husbands spoke in loud, blustering voices.

The men were gathered under the wisteria-choked trellis so they could smoke in peace, away from the women and restless babies. The women remained under the almond trees, teasing each other, laughter punctuated by sighs.

"Poor Antigone," one said, turning to look at Lydia's mother. "Ach, why can't men stay put where God saw fit to place them?"

"You said it!" Lydia's cousin put in. "Who can understand men?" She said this with her eyes on Antigone, but her mind, Lydia sensed, was on her own alcoholic husband.

And another, her aunt Koula, rocked her baby and said, "They come once a year and give us children, then—" She flicked the air, as if shooing a fly.

"They're gone again!" Lydia understood the gesture, its bitterness and its resignation: both Koula's father and her husband were merchant sailors.

Lydia stayed close, listening.

Then her aunt, Marianthi, her father's sister, spoke up.

"Ach, Koula," she said, sighing. "You've always been a grump. At least you have two healthy sons. Look at me: thirty-six years old and still childless. Barren as—" she turned, pointing with her chin, "—this old almond tree." Marianthi wiped a tear, hugging Lydia against her large, buxom body.

"Oh, look!" Lydia blurted out. "Nikos is playing with mud again!" She jumped off her aunt's lap and ran toward her two-year-old cousin, swiping at his blue sailor's suit. "Naughty boy! Naughty, naughty boy!"

She had succeeded in extricating herself from her aunt's embrace, but Marianthi's bitterness left its mark. Over the years, after she'd had her abortion, and then again during her miscarriage, Lydia would sometimes find her thoughts travelling back to her barren aunt, who had lost her mind during menopause—from pure disappointment, said the neighbours.

Lydia's musings were interrupted by the arrival of Dr. Seager, who examined her again, gloved hand probing her mangled flesh.

"I still can't pee on my own," she said, though the transparent drainage bag spoke for itself.

He sighed, "You mustn't worry. None of this is serious. We'll try a new medication on you." He spoke very gently while she lay, resigned, feeling her breasts swell with a superfluous substance. She had finally told him about her engorged breasts, surprised to learn that she had in fact been given a lactation suppressant right after delivery.

"Why isn't it working then?" she asked. "What's the matter with me?"

Seager spread his hands. "Nature can be stubborn. We'll give you new tablets."

"More tablets?"

"Might as well—they're on special this week." He grinned, rueful, then patted her hand, saying there was something he felt they should probably look into: the possibility of a genetic factor. "We'll do blood tests on both of you...you are still young enough..."

Lydia registered only fragments of what Dr. Seager was saying, for one word kept echoing in her head: *genetic*. So, likely or unlikely, it could still be that; there could still be an explanation.

"Unfortunately, the results won't be back for at least two weeks. You'll be home in time for the weekend, though," he added. "Meanwhile, try to get some exercise. Doctor's orders!"

After he left, a gaunt, elderly cleaner came in. Lydia achieved a vaguely friendly expression. The cleaner reminded her of her father, though he might have been Portuguese or Italian. She watched him empty her wastebasket. So many tissues! Pink and blue, crumpled and stained. Was there another room on this entire ward where so many tears had been shed?

The old man replaced the basket and their eyes met briefly. He smiled, then hastened to look away, as if caught in some impropriety.

He resembled a scarecrow, she thought, one badly shaken by too many storms. Soon, he trotted out, not quite shutting the door behind him. Lydia became aware of baby carts rolling down the long corridor; the wheels approaching, pausing briefly here and there to let mothers have their babies. Just outside Lydia's door, an infant was beginning to fret. Suddenly, there was a loud, masculine voice.

"Don't tell me!" A stranger laughed. "That's my son right there! Only kid ever born sounding like Mary's little lamb!"

"Lamb? That's hilarious!" A nurse giggled.

The fretting baby did sound like a lamb, but Lydia raised her hands and stuck her fingers in her ears. She did not quite succeed in shutting out the infant's cries, but soon both baby and father fell silent. The carts outside rolled on past Lydia's private room, down the long, bustling corridor, toward the waiting mothers.

26

When they first saw the house on Côte-Sainte-Catherine Road and Lydia worried that it might be too big, John reminded her that she had once talked about having three children. At least three!

"You can have half a dozen now, if you like," he recalled saying, pleased with their good fortune, happy to have made his wife laugh.

One day, when they had yet to move in, Lydia told him how, when she was a young teenager, she would go for long walks out of her family's poor neighbourhood and often pass by this very house.

"I used to wonder who lived in these houses—mansions, that's how I thought of them." Her laughter echoed through the empty rooms, which were just then being restored and painted. "I guess I'll have to get used to living like a princess."

John chuckled at that. He genuinely believed their new house would make his wife happy, once she got used to the upgrade. And in this he had turned out to be right.

Ironically, as the years went by, he himself began to find all those rooms a little oppressive, at least whenever he happened to be alone. Lydia belonged to a book club, which met once a month; occasionally, she took evening courses (music appreciation, film criticism, Szechuan cooking); once a week or so, she went to see her family. John spent hours alone in his study, reading surgical and scientific journals and, when he was tired, history or science fiction.

This afternoon, though, there was no time or inclination to sit down and read. He had come home from St. Margaret's to pack up the baby's things, as Lydia had requested, though he had a plan he decided to keep to himself. The plan depended on his mother's cooperation. He was counting on her to agree because it would enable him to keep everything they had purchased without Lydia having to face painful reminders on returning home.

There had been no answer at his parents' home when he tried to phone from the office, but there was no time to lose. He had stopped at a supermarket to get cardboard boxes and a bottle of wine for his parents. The boxes were fortunately kept flat and he was able to leave with an adequate stack.

Arriving at home before noon, he kept stumbling upon Lydia's things wherever he turned: cosmetics in the bathroom, a silk scarf wrapped around the bedroom's door knob, an old book she had picked up at some garage sale, lying face down in the living room.

He tried his mother again, but found her still out, as was Lorenzo, their ever-obliging Italian handyman. John continued to pack, though he was feeling exceptionally tired and also a little feverish. He stopped in the kitchen just long enough to down a cup of NeoCitran, then took a hot shower and lay down to have a nap.

When he awoke, shortly before five, he was surprised to find himself feeling almost restored. He showered again and shaved and made himself a cup of coffee. Out in the garden, the rain fell on the reddening trees, the still-green front lawn strewn with fallen leaves. It was windy and almost dark now. The cats were chasing each other up and down the long hallway.

The phone rang and there was his mother, finally returning his call.

"Your secretary said you were sick. What's the matter, do you have fever?"

He told her he didn't; all he had was a stuffy nose. He sat down with the phone, explaining about the baby furniture. He knew her house was crowded, he said, but could she possibly try to make a little space in the basement?

"Oh." A martyred sound accompanied this utterance. "Lydia's so impulsive! Can't you lock the door? It's a big house. She doesn't have to go into the nursery, does she?" Because he knew her well, John sensed in his mother's tone the unvoiced thought that Lydia should consider herself a lucky woman instead of giving in to what his mother liked to call "caprice."

"Oh, Mama," he said, "I'm sure you could find a bit of space somewhere, couldn't you? I don't know what else I can—"

She cut in roughly. "But it's nonsense! She'll get used to it—once she gets home. You know Lydia," she added.

For some reason these words made John want to hurt her. He said, "Lydia feels that you don't love her—that's why she doesn't want to see you."

There was a stunned silence, then an ambiguous little sound, followed by a heavy sigh John could not quite decipher. "Ach, Holy Virgin!" his mother said at length. "What children put their poor parents through these days."

Her voice was tearful, though this was something she was given to saying rather often, especially when speaking to her own daughter. John experienced a spurt of shame.

"Please, Mama," he said in a conciliatory tone. "She's not herself, you know. Postpartum hormones can drive a woman crazy, even with...a normal birth." He paused. "And it isn't just you...she doesn't want to see her own family either."

"Poor child," his mother said then. "I suppose I'll have to find room for that stuff—God only knows where though."

"Would you ask Lorenzo to come pick it up, please?"

"Do I have a choice?"

John let out a sigh of relief. It was a load off his mind, he told his mother. "I feel better already," he added.

He had told Lydia he would come by in the early evening. He was genuinely grateful to have his mother's cooperation, though he could have probably gotten her to agree on the spot simply by saying *he* wanted the stuff out of the house. This knowledge had perhaps been there in the back of his mind all along.

He said goodbye and made his way up to the bedroom to get dressed. He could hear Mrs. Farquhar, their widowed neighbour, puttering in the adjacent garden and, somewhere in his own house, the cats rolling their catnip ball on the hardwood floor.

He was a careless dresser. Unless Lydia intervened, he often went out inadequately dressed (both his wife and mother thought it no small wonder that he should catch colds so often). Today, though, he went about choosing his clothes carefully: wool socks, a new turtleneck, a blazer under his Burberry.

Everything he put on that day had been purchased by Lydia. She often bought him clothes, saying she had seen this or that on sale. Her obsession with sales irritated him, as did all her regressions to her impoverished childhood. She owned fine gold and silver jewellery and diamond earrings, but would seldom buy so much as a t-shirt unless it was on sale.

John had at some point given up protesting though. He had worked hard all his life, never expecting his wife's frugality to cast a small shadow on his professional success.

Nevertheless, the clothes were invariably well chosen. His wife, John grudgingly conceded, had much better taste than anyone in his own family. Better, certainly, than his mother, who sometimes bought him things of good, if somewhat flashy, quality. Lydia always chose muted colours; he rather liked that. Right now he was dressed in shades of brown and beige with just a hint of apricot in the knit of his sweater. Standing before the mirror, he put on an olive-green scarf she had brought one day from an arts and crafts fair.

It came to him that he wanted to please his wife, though he had almost forgotten her last-minute request to bring her journal when he visited next time. Her journal and a pen. She had a fine Montblanc fountain pen he had bought her one Christmas and she seemed to cherish it. Upon reflection, though, she'd told him someone might steal it while she was sleeping. "Just bring me a couple of regular ballpoints then."

"All right. I will."

It was a simple request, but one that had left John feeling oddly grateful. At least there was something he could do for her. Something she still cared about.

27

She must send him home when he comes back later. Why should he stay when he was so obviously ill at ease whenever he came? And why should she want him to, sensing he couldn't wait to get away—if not from her, then at least from the entire maternity ward? He would never admit it, of course, possibly not even to himself. And anyway, did he really love her? She knew he loved her body—or just desired it, how was she to know? But what was her body to him now but a bloated, bloody mass of wounded flesh that, for all his trouble, had produced nothing. Nothing!

Don't be silly now.

This was what he would likely say if she were to voice these feelings. It was something he was given to saying, especially over the worries she'd expressed during her pregnancy. It had never particularly bothered her; the words were not uttered without affection.

Waiting for John to arrive, though, Lydia's thoughts wandered, landing on one bitterly cold night, on which she'd found herself, for the first time that she could remember, recoiling from her husband's touch.

It happened soon after her pregnancy had been confirmed. The gynaecologist had said nothing about abstaining from sex and she herself had been too shy to ask. But she did voice her anxiety on that frigid mid-January night, and John had reacted as she might have known he would.

"You're being silly, Lydia—you know that, don't you?" Pressing his lean, hard body against her unwilling flesh, while she protested. "No, no—not yet, John—please, not yet."

The physical aversion continued unabated throughout the first trimester. Again and again, John brushed her worries aside, but never quite succeeded in dissipating the stubborn reluctance of her flesh. She hated him, in those first three months. His humorous condescension, his sexual power. She found herself sympathizing with her younger sister, who had recently announced that she was turning her back on men and moving in with a lesbian actress.

And then, quite suddenly, the physical loathing vanished, though a small dread lingered in the months that followed. She had tried to voice it several times: Was it quite safe, absolutely safe—at this point, in this position, such and such month? There were, she'd read, differences in medical opinion.

Some doctors recommended abstention, at least in risky pregnancies. She still could not bring herself to ask Dr. Minnaar, but made it a point to read everything she could lay her hands on.

It was, she eventually told her husband, considered by some to be a little risky toward the end of the pregnancy. "It can precipitate early labour for one thing, did you know that?" Her girth was by then a bit of an obstacle but also, perhaps, a challenge.

"Nonsense," said John, planting a kiss at the base of her neck. "There's only one rule I've ever heard: do what you can when you can!"

This was what her husband, the doctor, had said. But, waiting for him to arrive at the hospital on that Thursday evening, these all-but-forgotten words suddenly went careening through Lydia's brain. She could not wait to share these latest thoughts with her journal.

Could it be his fault then? Would we have lost the baby if he had deigned to listen to me?

FRIDAY
September 6, 1991

28

It was a busy morning but all his scheduled surgeries had been cancelled, so the early afternoon found Dr. John Gabriel free again for about two hours. He had to see two new patients at three and four o'clock, but there was something he needed to do before that.

Yesterday, gobsmacked by Lydia's emotional onslaught, he had driven down to Claire's despite all his qualms, hoping only for a cup of tea and some sympathy. To think that Lydia was now blaming him for the stillborn child! To think that he went to see her full of good will, only to be accused of selfishness, of caring more about sexual gratification than about his own unborn son!

He'd left St. Margaret's as soon as he decently could and headed downtown. Having resolved never to sleep in Claire's bed again, he had left her before midnight, forgetting his reading glasses. He was more than a little dismayed by this latest evidence of his chaotic mental state, as if it presaged early-onset dementia. He was not yet forty, yet his vision had begun to blur when he was barely thirty-five, he was beginning to suffer from hypertension, and his hair all at once had more grey in it than black. What was happening to him suddenly? Was he going to be an old man way before his time? The thought weighed heavily on his mind. His distant vision was still 20/20 but he couldn't so much as read a prescription without his reading glasses.

If he bought a sandwich in the coffee shop, and ate it while driving, he could make it to Claire's and back in plenty of time for his afternoon appointment. He had tried to call her twice from his office, but had only managed to reach her answering machine. She must be writing again. She had finally figured out what was wrong with her fictional character, she'd cheerfully announced last night.

Artists!

John was vexed with himself for having to disturb Claire again but he had no choice, since she was taking the train to Toronto later this afternoon. He hoped that she was not, at the last moment, getting her hair done or picking up clothes from the cleaners. How stupid of him to forget his glasses! He blamed it on the bit of weed she'd made him smoke yesterday evening, assuring him it would not only help him unwind but probably cure his cold symptoms as well.

This memory was accompanied by an inner sneer. The weed had done nothing to cure his cold, but had left him feeling vaguely unsettled. His mother had once told him he was too self-absorbed, but was he also a bit of a prig, as Claire had said after the weed had loosened her tongue? For the first time in his life, John Gabriel found himself contemplating the thought that he might be a rather repressed individual. Was he? Were there other things about himself he was unaware of?

He asked himself these questions, but quickly cast them aside as he parked his car, surprised to see Syd Gurman coming out of Claire's condominium building, pausing briefly to wipe his sunglasses, then walking briskly toward his parked Merc. John, stepping out of his own BMW, was about to hail Gurman, but how would he explain his own presence in Old Montreal at this time of day? And anyway, who knew what Syd was doing here during working hours?

Claire's heritage building had once been a cold-storage warehouse but had recently been converted into upscale condos and professional offices, the elegant Italianate façade restored, the high-ceiling flats revamped and refurbished. There was an architectural firm on the first floor and a divorce lawyer's office facing the port.

John took the elevator to the third floor. He rang Claire's bell, taken aback when she opened it almost instantly, saying: "What did you forget?"

Without thinking, he said, "My reading glasses." And then he stopped and looked at her closely, aware that she had suddenly paled.

John was not a suspicious man; he was indeed quite possibly naive, for it was not until he had closed the door and faced Claire's dining area that the obvious hit him, taking his breath away.

For what he was staring at was the irrefutable evidence of a recently consumed lunch: two plates with crumpled napkins, two glasses, an open bottle of wine. And flowers: a tall bouquet of purple irises that had certainly not been there last night.

Briefly, John closed his eyes, breathing deeply through his mouth. He then made straight for the living room, where he had left his prescription glasses, painfully aware of his thudding heart. The cushions on the sofa looked as neat as ever; his glass case was exactly where he had left it, on the stack of Claire's magazines. If she had not been in a rush, she would have probably seen it and called his office.

He hastened out of the sitting area and stood staring at her, poised against the large, sun-filled window. She usually wore jeans at home, but was now dressed in a short, cinnamon-hued skirt and matching blouse with a long row of buttons. John had a sudden vision of Syd Gurman unfastening all those tiny black buttons. A pathetic question followed this disconcerting vision: would he have managed it any faster—Gurman, with his short thick fingers that took two hours to do a cholecystectomy when he himself had done it numerous times in barely an hour?

"Stop looking at me with those inquisitor's eyes," Claire said. "All we did was have lunch, for christ's sake." She sighed, dropping into one of her decorative chairs and fidgeting with her necklace. John looked at the silver necklace, the open top buttons, and something gave a little lurch within him. He drew a long breath. Slowly, he raised his eyes and surveyed Claire.

"Lunch with Syd Gurman? But why?"

"Why not?" She shrugged. She crossed her shapely long legs.

John almost said, "Well, for one thing he's married to Beatrice." He stopped himself in time, thinking he was losing his marbles. "He's not exactly prince charming." Gurman was a tall, corpulent man with a balding head and perpetual squint.

"Who said I was looking for prince charming?"

"Well," he said, "What *are* you looking for? A Surgeon-in-Chief?" Would he have minded quite so much had it been someone else? John asked himself, his body clenched for her answer.

But she was smiling at him and there was, he thought, a hint of malice in that quirky smile. "I'm not especially in need of anyone," she said, "but...I have my reasons. I won't hold a man's professional success against him, that's for sure."

John glared at her. "I want to believe you have good reasons—I would be perfectly willing to believe you if you hadn't told me you were planning to spend the morning working...had you answered the phone when I tried to reach you."

Claire made a disgruntled gesture. "Things come up—plans change. Not everything is etched in stone for me, the way it is for you."

"What could come up between midnight and noon?" he demanded. "On a day when you're supposed to be going away. You suddenly realized you were short of weed for your trip or something? Is he your secret dealer? *What?*"

She smiled once more. "You're quite funny when you're angry."

"Oh," he said, "but not amusing enough when I'm my usual calm self, is that it?"

"You're never calm," she said, then amended it: "Hardly ever."

"So, is that why you've suddenly started seeing Gurman? Or have you seen him before?" he demanded.

Claire's expression suddenly altered. She looked up, her eyes blazing. "What is this? An interrogation?" she asked, her tone hardening. "What right have you got to stand there when—"

He cut her off, his head threatening to explode. "When I'm not even your husband, I know, but—"

"Even if you were my husband," she interrupted in turn, "do you think you could just stand there like a fucking inquisitor?"

John was silent. He rubbed his eyes, trying to efface the image of Gurman and Claire flirting over lunch. "Just answer this one question: are you lovers?" he asked quietly.

"No."

"Are you planning to take him on?"

"You said one question," she spat out, her face stiffening.

"So you are," he said, a wave of futility beginning to wash over him. He coughed, wiped his nose, licked his badly chapped lips. "What I don't understand," he said after a long silence, "is how a woman can spend an evening with one man, kiss him goodnight, then have a tête-à-tête with another one the very next morning. I just don't get it."

But Claire held his gaze. "I never asked you how you could sleep with me, then go right back to your good little wife, did I? *She* never asked you that, did she?"

John was suddenly at a loss for words. A vein in his temple throbbed. "Well, I'm sure she would if she knew," he answered lamely.

"And what would you say?" Claire asked, taunting him now.

He thought about it, or at least tried to, but a hazy feeling was settling over him; the sensation of rising fever. "I'd say—I don't know what I'd say," he let out, hoping to redeem himself with the plain truth.

"Well, maybe you should be asking *yourself* some questions, instead of flashing your censorious light on me," she said.

And what could he say to that? John brought his handkerchief up to his nose. "I thought you said I was too analytical," he said scornfully.

"You are," she said, a snap in her eye. "But for all that, you're not really in touch with your own emotions. You think and you analyze and you agonize, yet you're constantly pulling the wool over your own eyes."

This speech astonished John almost as much as the fact of Gurman's visit. He had always thought of himself as a man in search of the truth, one determined to confront his own demons, whatever it took. What he found more difficult just now was confronting his mistress. He felt torn between an intense desire to flee, and a simultaneous curiosity about whatever it was she was still withholding.

"What have I been deceiving myself about?" he asked, his eyebrows knitted together. "What?" he insisted when she kept her silence.

"What's the point?" she finally said. She glanced at her watch, and then at the window. "I have to pack," she said frostily.

"Is that why you sent *him* packing so quickly?" he said before he could stop himself. "Because you have a train to catch? Would you—"

"Look," she said, her voice all at once dangerously tight. "I told you: I'm not your wife—I won't have you talking to me like this, understand?" She folded her arms over her chest, her lips tightening.

"Lydia would never behave like this," he said. "Even if we were not married, she wouldn't."

"Well, bully for you!" Claire said. "You're a lucky chap!" Her mouth curled with scorn. "So why don't you run along now, back home like a good boy should. I'm sure she'll forgive you." She gave a short, rather unpleasant laugh.

John felt his hackles rise. He began to turn away, still clutching his glasses. "I wish I could be as sure as all that," he said, more or less to himself.

"Oh, you can be sure," said Claire, following on his heels. "What's more, it's your wife's greatest charm."

This stopped John in his tracks. "You're a bitch, Claire," he said, relishing the sound of a word he could not remember ever using before. "I don't need—"

"No, you certainly don't need me," she interjected with a smug little smile. "What you need is a shrink. Someone who'll get paid for listening to your tedious ramblings."

John forgot to breathe. He forced himself to stand perfectly still because, for the first time in his life, he knew how it felt to want to hit someone. The thought shocked him.

"If that's how you feel, so be it," he said, willing himself to remain calm. "But I don't understand: what have you been doing with me all this time?"

She forced a half-smile. "Getting to know you," she said, still toying with her necklace. They were standing in the foyer now, once more facing the dining room.

"You've known me for months now," he said, relishing his aversion. "More than seven, to be exact. A lot of time to waste on a tedious lover," he added with a scoffing sound. "Or have you just been collecting material for your novel?"

He had spoken sarcastically, had been all but ready to leave, but Claire looked so stunned suddenly that John could not help thinking he may have inadvertently hit the nail on its head.

The thought seemed shocking, monstrous, but he no longer cared. He was desperate to be out of there, in the fresh air, the afternoon sunlight. He felt like the bewitched prince in one of the fairy tales Lydia had bought for their unborn son, a book whose gorgeous illustrations she had shown him one warm summer evening. A prince who had at last broken the evil spell. His hand was already on the doorknob when he spun around.

"I despise you," he said, very evenly, "I've never really known what it is to hate anyone before." He opened the door, but not before seeing one corner of Claire's mouth lift ironically.

"I believe you," she said. "Men love women who forgive them more than their mothers ever could."

And then, at last, he was gone. And, astonishingly, the world outside went about its usual business, as intent and impervious as a swarm of bees buzzing around a honeycomb.

29

There was a knock at the door.

"Good afternoon."

Dr. Seager came in, looking pale and drawn. The skin was puffy around his eyes; one of his eyelids drooped. A wave of tender solicitude swept over Lydia.

"Were you up all night?"

"Yes."

She thought: delivering babies. She drew a long breath and closed her eyes. He was gazing at her intently.

"Things a little rough today?"

She nodded. "Why are the stitches suddenly so sore?"

"It's just the swelling around the episiotomy. It'll start getting better tomorrow—I promise."

He was going away for the weekend but would have the chief resident examine and discharge her if all went as expected.

All Lydia said was, "I see." But she knew that he'd seen her flinch when he said he was going away, leaving her in an unknown resident's hands. If they discharged her on the weekend, she might never see him again.

He looked at her closely. "Try to get involved with something when you get out of here."

"What?" she said bitterly. "Ladies' Auxiliary?"

"Anything to keep your mind off yourself." He slid his stethoscope into his pocket, taking in the paperback she had borrowed from the mobile volunteers' cart: *When Pregnancy Fails*. "Come on," he said with sudden resolve. "Let me help you up. I want you to go for a walk."

He helped her slide off the bed, but she said she needed to go to the bathroom first, so he said goodbye and left the room, wishing her a speedy recovery.

She sat on the toilet for a while, then stepped out into the corridor and trudged toward the nursing station, mulling over Dr. Seager's advice. What could she possibly do to keep her mind off herself?

The question got tossed in her mind for a while, stirring up an exchange she'd had with John back in December, a few weeks before discovering that she was pregnant. She had been thinking of enrolling in an art history course starting in January, but he talked her into taking creative writing instead.

"Just think," she recalled him saying. "You may someday walk into a library and find a book with your own name on it. Wouldn't that be exciting?"

His comment had made Lydia flush with pleasure, but the thought of writing a book, she told him the next morning, made her feel like a plain girl yearning to become a movie star. All the same, she finally allowed herself to be persuaded. She registered for the winter session, but dropped out almost immediately, after finding herself pregnant soon after New Year's.

Picking her way down the long hospital corridor, Lydia was still mentally flipping through various options when something stopped her in her tracks.

Outside the nursing station, wrapped in pastel blankets, half a dozen babies were laid out in tiny cots, waiting to be claimed by their mothers. Most of the infants were asleep, small ID bracelets dangling from their fragile wrists. There was a bright lounge off the nursing station and, as she passed it, Lydia saw the mothers, dressed in street clothes now, getting last-minute instructions from Mrs. Atkinson.

They are taking their babies home.

She must not think about them, must cast aside the heavy stones that kept threatening to drag her down. She must make an effort, or she would be lost.

She stood frozen for a spell, holding her hand to her chest in a gesture of distress she had picked up from her mother. At that moment, an infant in one of the cots gave a short, tentative cry, then began howling, his tiny, clenched fists shaking in the air, his face turning purple.

Lydia's own hands had also begun to tremble. She looked toward the nurse on duty, who was on the phone, writing something on a pad; then, again, at the mothers in the lounge. The new mothers were all intent on Mrs. Atkinson, who was busy demonstrating something. Lydia motioned to the nurse, but the head nurse only raised her hand like a traffic policeman, signalling her to wait.

Lydia waited. For one interminable moment she bent over the wailing infant, racked by anxiety and a distressed, violent longing. She was feeling unbearably hot, her armpits damp, her breasts starting to leak. She had become oblivious to her surroundings, even as an urgent voice kept hissing in her ear: "Don't! Don't you dare touch him!"

She almost did. She had leaned into the crib and was making small soothing sounds when a young nurse approached, wearing an indulgent smile.

"Oh, is he yours?"

"No," Lydia hastened to say. "No...I was just passing. He seemed—"

"Oh, you're a real go-getter, aren't you? Aren't you?" the girl crooned, taking the shrieking infant into her arms. "Between you and me, you're lucky," she told Lydia in a whispered aside. "This one's gonna keep his mama hopping, I can tell you that!" She turned away, cradling the frantic baby. "I guess we'll have to go find your mama, won't we?"

Lydia offered something resembling a smile. She padded back to the bathroom, where she found a cleaner mopping the floor; then all the way to the distant lounge, only to find it occupied by two chatty mothers; and then back, up and down the long immaculate corridor, thinking feverishly, doing her best to ignore the sharp blade scraping across her heart.

Is there any place, anywhere in this world, for a mother with empty arms?

SATURDAY
September 7, 1991

30

"There must be a lot of anger at a time like this."

Helen was sitting across from her brother. She had dropped in without calling just before lunch and found John in pyjamas and slippers, nursing his cold. They had lunch together—alone for the first time in years—then moved to the living room, away from the noise of their neighbour's lawn mower.

Mrs. Farquhar's son and his family had come for their annual visit and her twin grandsons were out, helping with domestic chores. John made iced tea. It was a humid day, but the living room, shaded by an enormous old poplar, had the cool, hushed atmosphere of a mountain retreat. Occasionally, a soft breeze came through the raised window; sparrows and chickadees sang in the leafy branches.

"I imagine one of the hardest things," said Helen, "is having no one to blame when something like this happens." She gazed at her brother with doleful eyes. "Poor Yannaki," she said. It was the diminutive for Ioannis, his Greek Christian name.

John heaved a sigh. His eyes fastened on the pale nineteenth-century silk screen hanging on the living room wall. "Poor Yannaki feels that he is to blame."

He had, alone at home since yesterday afternoon, done nothing but dwell on the past nine months, the past eleven years. And though he had, over lunch with his sister, confessed his ambivalent feelings toward the unborn child, he could not shake his nagging sense of guilt.

It was over with Claire. He knew this much, but was sufficiently self-aware to acknowledge that, for all his wounded pride, Claire had been right about some rather significant things. He was grateful to be in the company of his sister, even if she thought that blaming oneself for the stillbirth was just one way of denying the randomness of fate.

"You've always had trouble accepting this," she reminded him at length. "But some events are...quite simply beyond our control."

"Oh, Helen," he said wearily. "Please—no philosophy today." John thrust his head between his hands. "I don't think I've ever felt so wretched in my entire life. Everywhere I turn, I see nothing but ruins."

She looked at him steadily. "Lydia's going to need someone to lean on when she comes home, you know." There was a faintly reproachful edge to his sister's voice, but perhaps he imagined it?

"I know," he said and pressed his lips together. "You're right."

Helen got up and went to the window, smoothing down her Mexican summer dress. She stood for a moment, staring out at the yellowing poplar, its branches stirring in the afternoon breeze. Sappho came into the room and rubbed against Helen's bare legs.

"May I use the bathroom?"

"You'll have to go upstairs." The downstairs toilet did not flush properly. "Everything seems to be breaking down since Lydia left," said John. "Not that she would have tried to fix any of it," he added, almost smiling. "The kitchen—this great kitchen she herself designed—has always been her kingdom. She won't even change the washer on a dripping faucet."

Helen chuckled, then headed for the stairs while John downed his tea, his mind wandering. He thought it a pity that, despite all her achievements, Lydia's confidence did not extend beyond the culinary realm. When he compared her to Claire, which he couldn't help doing right now, it seemed obvious to him that while his wife might not be as adventurous or as witty, she was at least as intelligent, and perhaps even more naturally gifted than his erstwhile mistress.

All at once, John found himself plunged deep into resentment for Claire's inflated self-regard. He waited for Helen, staring out the window. It came to him then that he hadn't fed the fish since yesterday when he'd come home to help Lorenzo load all the baby stuff onto his truck. At least he had solved that problem.

In the solarium, John opened the aquarium and shook some flakes into the water, as he had been instructed. At once, the fish came swimming to the surface and began snapping at the food. John blew his nose, staring into the tank for a moment before returning to the living room.

And then the phone rang and it was—as he had somehow known it would be—Lydia. He still felt guilty for coming down with the flu and being unable to go and see her yesterday. They had discussed the possibility, should he fail to get better, of her going to stay with her mother, where the caretaker was still on full-time duty. Lydia had said she would think about it.

"You weren't napping, were you?" she asked the moment he answered the phone.

"No. I was...just feeding the fish as a matter of fact. I forgot to do it this morning." John sighed, returning to the living room. "I'm sorry."

"How are you feeling?" she asked.

"I seem to be getting better. Temperature's normal for now." He ran his hand through his hair. "I thought I might come later and—"

"Absolutely not," Lydia said, cutting in firmly. "The last thing we need is to have you spreading germs around the maternity ward. Anyway, they're getting ready to discharge me." She paused, started to add something, then seemed to think better of it. There was a prolonged silence. John heard a door open and close on the second floor. Helen was descending the carpeted stairs. He was still trying to decide whether he should tell Lydia that his sister was there when he suddenly sneezed. He said, "Hold on a minute, will you?"

He put the phone down and blew his nose. He could hear Helen address one of the cats in the hallway. And then she dropped something just outside the entrance to the living room.

Lydia's voice said, "Hello? Are you still there, John?"

John coughed, covering the phone. "I'm here." He motioned Helen to keep quiet.

"What's going on?" said Lydia.

"Nothing, darling," he said. "Nothing." He thought it best not to tell her. Lydia had made it clear she was not yet ready to speak to anyone; had, in any case, always disliked talking on the phone. Although she loved Helen, he thought she would hate to have to talk to her on the phone just now, without adequate preparation. He rubbed his face, trying to decide what to do.

"John, you're not alone, are you?" When he took his time answering, Lydia added, "I know you're not." She sounded, all at once, on the verge of tears.

John took a deep breath and let it out slowly. "Helen's back. She dropped in. She was thinking of coming to see you. Would you like her to?"

"Helen!" There was a note of—what? Surprise, panic, relief? "Is she there right now?"

"Yes." Helen sat on the living room sofa, blinking uncertainly. "Would you like to speak to her?"

Lydia said, "Yes...no...I don't know!" Then fell silent, reacting exactly as he had predicted. She exhaled audibly. "Actually, I'd rather not, John—not on the phone." Would he ask Helen please to come see her at home in a couple of days, she asked in a halting voice. "I'm just not ready," she added with a heavy sigh. "You think she'll understand?"

"I'm sure she will." John looked up at his sister, shrugging. "Don't worry about it. Helen can wait," he added.

Lydia was silent for a moment. "How is she?"

"Helen? Terrific. Sturdy and dark as a *campesina*." Helen made a face in his direction. She looked like their father, with her big jaw and her close-set, melancholy eyes. "What's that?" he said into the telephone.

"Please say hi for me," Lydia said in a faraway voice. And then she made a rather odd sound, something between a snort and a hiccup. "I thought you had...some young chick with you."

"Oh, Lydia." John felt something scrape across his heart.

"I'm sorry. Tell Helen I'm sorry too, will you?"

"Yes. Yes, I will," He managed to get out. "I'll call you again a little later, okay?"

They said goodbye. John leaned back against the silk cushions, squirting nasal spray into his nostrils. "What did you drop?" he asked his sister.

"Huh?" Helen looked momentarily distracted; she had been leafing through one of the books on the coffee table. "Oh, just my bag. The strap keeps getting loose."

"I see." John chuckled. One of the things Helen was known for was her battered black shoulder bag, which she always had on her, full of unpredictable objects (African shells and empty matchboxes, hand lotion and panties, amber worry beads) and which, no doubt because of its weight, she always unloaded promptly and rather heedlessly: in front of an exquisite floral arrangement, on white Damask tablecloths, on a freshly-made bed. It was a habit that still made their mother roll her eyes and invoke the saints. All John felt was an amused tolerance: she would never be the conventional daughter his mother had always hoped for. He smiled across the coffee table, feeling his love for his sister.

He said, "Lydia heard you drop it. She thought I had my mistress with me." He shrugged deprecatingly.

Helen eyed him curiously. "Do you have a mistress?"

John began a negative nod of his head. Then stopped, dropped his gaze, put the tips of his fingers together. Could he confide in his own sister? He would have preferred not to, but she knew him too well, would quickly know he was lying. There was also a sudden need to unburden himself.

"I did, briefly. It's over now, anyway. For good."

"I see." Helen scooped Sappho into her arms, then sat back and stroked the purring Persian cat. John's eyes were fastened on the Imari pottery in the coffee table. It was an ancient hibachi handsomely converted to display these old pieces under transparent glass. "Do you want to talk about it?"

"I'm not sure." John raised his eyes, his nerves feeling jangled. Mrs. Farquhar's lawn mower had finally fallen silent, and now a baby could be heard, crying nearby. "It just ended yesterday, as a matter of fact, and—well, the truth is I'm still a little shaken." He said this, his ears burning at the memory of his final encounter with Claire. "I left her place feeling as if I'd been pushed down a flight of stairs or something. I wish I'd never met her. She was a bitch, really."

Helen pulled her heavy hair back and held it off her neck, her eyes on the open window. "I don't know what to say. I never thought I'd hear you use this word, let alone cheat on your wife."

John was quiet, waiting. He squirted more nasal spray, thinking *he* not only didn't know what to say, he did not know what to do in the coming days. Lydia would be home any day now, but he feared she might slide into depression, as she had after her miscarriage, all those years ago. Should he come clean to her about the affair with Claire? Honesty is the best policy, people liked to say, but wouldn't it be rather cruel to confess just now, given Lydia's fragile state?

Yes, he decided, it was really out of the question. For now, he would have to keep carrying the full weight of his guilt. Would it be possible to start a new chapter, though, given his shameful secret? Was it even reasonable to hope for a strong relationship, knowing that he had betrayed his wife at the worst possible time?

John stared into the distance, wishing he could share some of these thoughts with Helen. He could not imagine grappling with his guilt for the rest of his life. Someday, he would have to come clean to Lydia. Someday, when they were both on steadier ground, but not just now. Just now, all he could do was try to be the husband Lydia deserved.

The thought made John sigh though, having made up his mind, he felt the stirring of a fledgling hope. For some reason, he felt compelled to make one thing clear to his sister.

"I was never in love with Claire, you know."

Helen gave him an appraising look. "Well, thank God for small mercies."

Sappho jumped out of her arms and hunched on the window seat, making odd rattling sounds at a twittering sparrow. In the distance, someone revved up a motorbike and then was gone. There was sudden silence.

"So, why *did* you get involved with her?" Helen ventured.

"Oh, who knows?" John sagged against the cushions, letting out a small rueful sound. "I believe it's called mid-life crisis," he said and sighed. "Did you know I'll be turning forty next Monday?"

"Of course I know!" she said. "I have a present from Mexico for you." Sappho had come back. Helen stroked her head and burrowed into her neck, the fuzzy softness of her ear. The cat's eyes were tiny blue slits; she was purring furiously. Helen looked up at John. "Go on," she said.

"Well, it's all too banal for words: wife pregnant, husband feels neglected, beautiful woman comes along and...seduces him, I guess." But had she actually done that? Was he being fair? John stroked his nostrils, his eyes fixed on Helen's face. His sister was staring back at him, a line between her level grey eyes. Was she judging him?

"Lydia went off sex at one point," he said with averted eyes. "She seemed to think it might harm the baby." He shrugged.

"Was this the first time?" asked Helen.

"The first time I had an affair? Yes!" He looked at her for a long moment. "But...to be honest, it wasn't really about the sex." Claire happened to be a marriage counsellor; an insightful, rather brilliant woman, he explained haltingly. "I should have probably gone to see a shrink, but...well, she seemed willing to help me sort things out." He shrugged.

"Hm. I would have thought that having secret trysts was more likely to seriously complicate a few things," said Helen.

"Well, yes. In some ways, I guess. But—" John fell silent, thinking about his last night with Claire. "She did manage to shed light on several serious issues. One way or the other, I've had to confront some... hard truths. Mostly about myself."

"Like?"

"I'd always thought I'd be happier, a better husband, if I'd married a different sort of woman."

"A woman like Claire Remington." It was said matter-of-factly.

"Well, yes and no. A more...sophisticated woman, I guess; more self-assured, more...ambitious." He looked vaguely apologetic. It occurred to him for the first time that Lydia might have been more self-assured had *she* married a different sort of man. The thought made his heart feel bruised. If he spent the rest of his life making it up to his wife, it might still not be enough.

"And—?"

"And now I'm suddenly not sure anymore." He coughed into his hand. "Claire's such a...bloody hedonist."

"Hedonist?"

"Yes. She's so...hard-edged, you know? A cool, selfish bitch." He needed to say it again, he needed to get everything off his chest.

Helen took a long time to answer. John waited. He hoped that she was not going to be too hard on him. "Well, there aren't too many women like Lydia in this day and age," she finally said.

"No. No, there really aren't."

John suddenly remembered Helen, many years ago, speaking of Lydia's warm generosity, her enormous capacity for love. He thought of the things Claire had said to him yesterday, and others she had implied. Despite his inner turmoil, he saw one thing with perfect clarity: Lydia was an exceptionally good wife.

"The thing is," he said, "I think I may have been unconsciously angry because she ended up miscarrying when we came back from our honeymoon, you know? I felt..." He hesitated.

"That you got trapped into marrying her?"

"Yes. Something like that." John dropped his gaze. "I've even wondered if, you know, our...inability to have a child all those years had a psychological basis." He spread his hands—how was one to know? He had been thrilled when, sometime after Christmas, Lydia told him she was finally pregnant. He recalled that evening as one of their happiest as a couple.

"By then, I'd got used to her ways, I suppose—she'd changed, for one thing, after she went back to school, you know? I've read some of her writing recently and it really is amazing. And when you think that English is not even her mother tongue! She's naturally gifted, she really is."

Helen smiled gently, almost pityingly. "You don't have to tell me."

"Anyway…I was really happy about the child at first. We both were, but—"

"You began to have doubts."

"I did." John threw his head back and closed his eyes. He listened to Mrs. Farquhar's grandsons laughing on the lawn. They were in their early teens, two fair-haired identical twins playing with a Frisbee. John thought of all the furniture and toys in his mother's basement, then of the bright, empty nursery upstairs. His throat constricted.

"One thing I'm just beginning to accept is the impossibility of ever having all the answers," he said at length.

"All the answers! Little Yannaki's still looking for all the answers." Helen chuckled." Well, who knows, maybe forty will turn out to be the age of wisdom for my dear brother." She smiled and reached for her bag. "I've got to go soon," she said, "but listen to this for a moment." She picked up one of Lydia's books from the coffee table and began to read:

"Imagine this scene: three to four hundred people, strangers to each other, are told to pair up and ask their partner one single question. 'What do you want?' Over and over again. Could anything be simpler? One innocent question and its answer."

John made a small chortling sound. "Could anything be more complicated?"

"*Don't* let yourself complicate it!" said Helen. "Insist on a simple answer! What do you want?"

"I know the answer, but it isn't simple." John made a vaguely dismissive gesture. He did not care for books by pretentious psychotherapists.

"Well," she said, "you can go on playing your little cerebral games, or you can decide what you really want. It's up to you, you know, where you go from here."

"You don't understand," he insisted. "I know where I want to go now, I really do—I am just not sure how to get there." He sighed. This was the problem in a nutshell, he said to himself. This was what he had to work on.

He scratched his nose thoughtfully, gazing at his sister. They held each other's eyes for a while.

And then she flicked him an oddly familiar look; something he remembered seeing as a boy in his father's eyes, at once amused and rueful. Another moment and she was even quoting their father and the amusement was his.

"When you really want to get someplace," she said, "even a hay cart will eventually get you there."

"Is that a promise?" he asked.

"It's a promise."

31

She was told the chief OBS/GYN resident would come by a little later to examine her one last time and authorize Sunday's discharge. Her bladder function was finally normal and, as Dr. Seager had promised, the stitches were less painful. Her breasts, though, were still engorged. She felt tired and old and useless. A trapped fly buzzed against the window panes, pausing to rest every now and then before resuming its frantic efforts.

Lydia picked up the book she had borrowed, hearing strangers' voices in the corridor, thinking again of the friends and relatives she would sooner or later have to face. John had told her they'd telephoned; they all wanted to see her. She could not properly explain her persistent need to shut them out, did not think anyone could possibly understand her. She needed her husband to be her gatekeeper.

A kitchen aide came in with a breakfast tray, humming to herself. Barely glancing at Lydia, she set the tray down, then left with an air of haughty cheer, a faint fragrance of hairspray lingering in her wake.

Lydia forced herself to eat some apple sauce and a bit of yogurt. She picked at the dry corn flakes, then, sighing, downed some lukewarm coffee and went back to reading her book.

When Pregnancy Fails was turning out to be unexpectedly informative, confirming once and for all that her own strange reactions were entirely normal. Despite Seager's assurances, it was only after she'd read the personal anecdotes in the book that Lydia knew she was not alone. She felt a comforting sense of sisterhood, a tender intimacy she had searched for after her miscarriage and now felt, improbably, with American women she had never met. When John had asked whether there was anything he could do for her, she had come close to saying: Find someone who has been through this, someone I can talk to, who'll understand what I'm going through.

She arrived at a new chapter. There were nearly one million families experiencing birth tragedies every year. One million in the U.S. alone! What would it be in Canada? In Greece? In the whole world? Out in the corridor, there was the usual hubbub of happy families. But somewhere in Montreal, at that very moment, there had to be other women with empty arms, whom she could maybe contact? To whom she could cry: "Mine too! I had a son, and he died for some reason, just the other day!"

Lydia levered herself up and reached for her journal so she could jot down a name and address. She had, while first thumbing through the old paperback, come upon a list of international help organizations. She had not given it a thought at the time, but now perused the list with mounting interest. There seemed to be a branch in Toronto but none in Montreal. Could she herself start a local organization for bereaved mothers? Did she have the wherewithal to undertake such a task?

After a while, she opened the bedside drawer and once again took out her son's photograph, then the small envelope with its silky bits of black hair. She thought of the moment Emmanuel had been whisked away: a long-limbed, red-faced infant wrapped in a blue blanket. Cold as marble. She lay facing the window, intent on the trapped fly's frantic attempts to escape the room. Though the window was partially open, the fly kept circling the window, desperately flinging itself against the upper pane.

Lydia blew her nose, wishing herself elsewhere. When the kitchen aide came back for the breakfast tray, she pulled the sheet up to her chin, pretending to be asleep. Out in the hallway, two women chatted in a language she didn't understand, erupting now and then into peals of laughter. A bespectacled orderly or technician poked his head through the door, but promptly withdrew, muttering apologies.

Somewhere in the distance, an ambulance siren shrieked, growing ever louder.

Lydia found herself praying again, though she couldn't have said for what, exactly, and certainly not to whom.

SUNDAY
September 8, 1991

32

It had become their habit to have herbal tea after dinner, but usually it was Lydia who did the carrying and serving in the solarium. Today, John came in from the kitchen, bearing a tray with Lydia's favourite chocolates and a pot of mint tea. It was her first evening back home from the hospital. Lydia managed a wan smile. She watched wordlessly as her husband set the mugs on the glass coffee table. He poured the tea, then sat down with a sigh, pulling a rumpled handkerchief out of his pants pocket.

"I can't believe how much better I feel, now that you're home," he said, dabbing at this nose. "The fever's completely gone; I've just about stopped coughing. Amazing!"

He leaned back in his armchair and replaced his handkerchief, warming his hands on the Japanese teacup. The aquarium pump made a gentle, gurgling sound, like a running brook. John parted his lips to add something, then stopped himself and sat for a moment, thoughtfully staring into his tea.

"I really missed you," he finally said. "The house seemed so empty without you." For a moment, their eyes met and held each other, then John's flickered and slid away. "Everything seemed to be going wrong without you. Every little thing."

Lydia released a long, melancholy breath. She smoothed back a white lock of hair, then sat in silence, eyes fixed on a giant fern suspended from the ceiling.

"What's the matter?" John asked at length. He looked at her closely. "Lydia?" He put down his pipe.

Something seemed to be happening to her face. It was as if her features were struggling to find the appropriate expression. Any moment, she might burst into tears—or laughter. But all she did was drop her gaze and shift her weight in the rocking chair. Speaking in a toneless voice, she finally said, "I was thinking of leaving you."

"You were...thinking of leaving?!" John echoed weakly. He sat up and stared at Lydia with dilated eyes. "Oh, dear God," he muttered at length. He then slid into silence, rubbing his face frantically, as if trying to pull off a clinging mask.

Another moment passed. John looked at Lydia again and let out one of his deepest sighs. "You were not yourself, you know, my dear," he finally said. "Neither of us was."

Lydia opened her mouth to speak, then closed it without uttering a word. Despite occasional crying jags, she looked much better than she had for days. There were still shadows under her eyes, but her hair had been washed and there was a trace of colour on her lips. She seemed to be making an effort.

"I didn't think you'd really care," she finally let out. She dodged John's eyes, letting her look pause on the fish gliding in the aquarium. "The worst of it is...I'm not even sure why I wanted to leave, exactly." She looked stricken, suddenly. "One minute I thought it was because you didn't love me, next because I imagined I could...I thought I might have a normal pregnancy with...you know, someone else."

They were still waiting for the genetic test results, but John visibly flinched.

"Lydia!" He sat for a moment, barely breathing, while she began to cry, her gaze fixed on the ceiling. "You actually thought of marrying someone else," he said, sounding dazed.

Lydia tugged at her sleeve. "Yes," she said. Arion had just come in, jumping into her lap. Lydia's kimono fell open at the neck, exposing her opulent flesh. She sat stroking the Siamese cat's lean back. The antique Seikosha wall clock in the hall struck eight. "I thought you didn't really want to have a child."

John bent forward and put his face in his hands. He coughed a little, then sat drinking desultorily, his eyes on the bouquet of red roses his mother had sent to welcome her daughter-in-law home. Lydia had set the flower vase on an old pine cabinet, next to the urn containing their son's ashes. In front of the urn, she had placed Emmanuel's photograph. John was staring at it now, forcing himself not to avert his eyes.

"Well," he said after a while, "Truth to tell, you were not...not entirely wrong." He bowed his head, like a child forced to confess to a shameful act.

"I wasn't?" Lydia's hand went to her kimono collar, clutching it together, as if a window had suddenly been blown open. She looked at him, pale and impassive.

"There were times when, if I'm being honest, I wasn't sure I really wanted it," he said with a heavy breath. The words had come all measured out, tight with the effort of reluctant disclosure. "I was...terribly confused, you know. I really wasn't sure what it was I wanted." John tapped his pipe, then sat for a moment, his hand over his mouth.

"It's so...fucking complicated. Everything's so... bound up together." He fell abruptly silent, stopping to blow his nose. Lydia was sitting with her hand against her cheek, as if recovering from a slap. When she spoke, it was with an obvious effort.

"Did you not want to have a child...with me?"

"No, no," John said. "Nothing like that. Nothing like that!"

"Why then?" she asked, blinking across the coffee table. "All those years...I thought you wanted a baby. A lot."

"I did," he said, "I...do. Only—" He hesitated, running a hand through his unwashed hair. "Look, this has more to do with my own demons than with you. And it's...unbelievably difficult for me to suddenly let everything out, but please, *please* don't jump to conclusions, okay? I haven't quite worked it out myself. I need time." He sighed and compressed his lips. There was heavy silence.

"Time," Lydia echoed vaguely. She cradled her cup, her eyes searching his face. After a while she said, "I guess we don't have to talk about it right now if you don't want to."

"Actually, I do," said John. "I do. You might even—" He broke off and scratched his head; a deeper sigh escaped him. "I'd better go back and tell you something... something I should have got off my chest... months ago." He paused again, rubbing his nose. "I— about the time you found out you were pregnant—I learned I was not going to be replacing Abramson."

Lydia raised her eyes and regarded him for a spell. A baffled look took over her features. "I didn't even know you were hoping to make Chief," she finally said.

"Well, I was." John dabbed at his nostrils. "Though I hadn't immediately admitted I was counting on it, not even to myself. Anyway, my chances were actually very good, but...to make a long story short, Syd Gurman got the job instead." The muscles in

John's face stiffened; he hesitated for the briefest of moments. "I'm sure I don't have to tell you who's the better surgeon—" he started, but almost at once lapsed into morose silence. Lydia got up and went to sit on the wicker loveseat beside him.

"Why didn't you tell me?"

"Oh, I don't know." John took her hand and stroked it, looking thoughtful. "You were so enraptured, so... absorbed in your pregnancy. You'd just found out a few days before and—" He faltered, closing his eyes. "This is so...difficult. Especially now," he added, shaking his head bleakly.

Lydia said nothing for a long, pensive moment.

"You must have been so disappointed," she said after a while.

"Oh, you have no idea," he said. "Though I didn't really understand it at the time, you know? I felt— this will seem childish to you—but I felt as if you, too, had...abandoned me. I was hurt, and kind of resentful, I guess, and...well, I suppose it all got translated into a sort of irrational hostility toward you and the baby." He turned and looked straight into her woeful eyes. "Am I making any sense?"

She did not speak at once. She was staring at the dark window, the flashing lights of a passing jet.

After a while she said, "When I was a child, I longed to have a set of colour crayons one of my classmates had received from American relatives.

This was back in Greece, right after Christmas. There was a drawing I wanted to do and she wouldn't share them, so I stole the crayons. I don't know whether I'd intended to keep them after I'd done my drawing. Anyway, the next day, I returned them because the teacher asked the class and...well, it seems I could steal but couldn't lie to a teacher I worshipped. I did the right thing, finally. I returned the crayons."

Lydia drew a breath, eyes hazy with reminiscence. She seemed to be talking to herself.

"After a while, though, I began to feel angry; angry and sort of...resentful, you know? My father had left for Canada, not long before Christmas, so that year there were no New Year's gifts for any of us." Lydia inclined her head. "Why should Olga have such nice colour crayons when everybody knew I was a better artist? That's what kept going through my head after...after I had secretly returned the crayons. No one knew I'd been the one to steal them, but one morning—it was days later but I still felt this intense resentment—I found a small doll Olga had forgotten in the playground and...I buried it on the beach. It wasn't much, really, just a silly little doll with badly matted hair, but I knew Olga was attached to it and—well, I'm ashamed of it to this day, but I really got a terrific sense of satisfaction burying that doll, knowing Olga would cry for it as I had for those lovely American crayons."

Lydia's left eyelid had begun to quiver. Slow, silent tears were rolling down her cheeks, though she had told her story in a slow, self-possessed voice. John looped his arm around her shoulders. He sat stroking her hair.

"Do you believe in God?" she asked after a while.

"What? You know I don't. Why?"

"Because I always say that I don't, yet I find myself addressing him, appealing to him when I'm really desperate...I have several times, in the past few days."

"Well, it's not so surprising. We've all been programmed to do it."

"I guess so, but it's more than that. I think...at bottom, I do believe in divine justice, you know?"

"There's no such thing," he said. "Even if there is a God, he's certainly not just."

"Maybe not. It's not rational, I guess, but a part of me seems to believe in retribution. I keep thinking I'm being punished for something I've done—some past, possibly forgotten, transgression. But all I keep coming up with are ridiculous things: the crayons, the stupid doll! I honestly can't think of anything worse I've ever done."

The statement made John exhale wearily. He was looking thoughtful, as if trying to process what he had just learned.

A long moment went by. Lydia shifted her weight. "I'm so glad you decided to talk to me," she finally let out. "I...always sensed there was something wrong, something negative in your feelings about the baby." A bitter sound escaped her lips. "I told myself I was imagining things."

"Oh, my darling!" John said, turning to kiss her cheek. "Can you—will you ever forgive me?"

Lydia sighed but did not answer; she seemed momentarily distracted. "This is so confusing," she said, as if speaking to herself. "It never occurred to me to feel sorry for you."

"Well, how could you?" said John. "It's hardly your fault, any of it. I kept trying to figure out what it was I actually wanted. It seemed to change from day to day." He paused, looking hopeless. "I don't know...I still can't make sense of some of it. I never used to question my own motives, I guess. Not until recently." His hand caressed the back of Lydia's neck while she sat with her hands knotted in her lap, staring at the fruit bowl. "Your tea's getting cold," he said.

"Yes, thank you." She reached for her cup, then looked up, scanning John's haggard features. "I must have been...really wrapped up in myself, I guess. After I got pregnant."

"Yes," said John, quickly adding, "Understandably."

A pause fell between them.

"Why did Gurman get the job?"

"Well." John shifted uneasily. "He's done some research, which I haven't."

"And that's important for a Chief Surgeon's position?"

"Apparently." John gave a deprecating shrug.

Lydia refilled their cups with fresh tea and handed one to her husband. Sappho joined Arion in one of the chairs. The two cats lay nestled on the corduroy cushion, licking each other energetically. Out on the street, a shrill car horn broke the evening silence. They drank their tea. John was quiet for a moment, chewing on his pipe.

"To be perfectly honest, though, I think there was something else," he said at length. "Something personal. I seemed to have some sort of ridiculous anxiety problem...the child not measuring up and all that."

Lydia was looking distracted. "I wonder how many children do measure up," she said absently. But then she seemed to rouse herself, adding: "Think of all the people we know whose kids have dropped out of school or are doing drugs, or—"

"Exactly." John sighed. "Exactly! Then you meet someone like my accountant who agonizes for years about adopting a child and ends up with a Rhodes scholar. Go figure."

Lydia remained silent. She watched the cats, which had stopped licking and lay buried in each other, purring audibly. Over in the corner, a small leaf detached itself from a weeping laurel and silently fell onto the faded kilim rug.

"It's...so hard—feeling optimistic about anything right now." Lydia sighed, her hand on her brow. "I am so tired all the time!" She checked her watch. "It's not even nine o'clock and I feel as if I've just been crushed by that falling beam at the stadium." The reference was to something she had heard on the local news: a fifty-five-tonne beam had crashed to the ground, shutting down Montreal's Olympic Stadium. Lydia shifted her weight, her hand sliding down to her breast. "My whole body's still sore."

John had been lost in his own musings, but now turned and gently rubbed Lydia's shoulder. "Why don't I run your bath for you?" he offered. "I bought you some Ombre Rose bath gel."

A flush of surprise spread over Lydia's face. "How sweet of you," she said. Ombre Rose was the perfume she had worn for years.

"I thought I'd better." John almost smiled. "Or you might go back to using the red bath hearts my mother has given you."

Lydia made an ambiguous sound, then slid off the loveseat and moved about languidly, examining her plants. The fern seemed in need of a good dunking; a few gardenia leaves had begun to yellow. She stopped before a frail octopus plant while John went about clearing the coffee table.

"I can't believe it!" said Lydia, bending over the plant. "I've had this thing for three months—my mother threw it out because it had died on her. It just wouldn't grow, not even with my green thumb!" She turned and looked at him with raised eyebrows. "I was ready to give up on it myself but look...it's finally growing a new set of leaves."

John came and looked over her shoulder. "Must be my magic touch," he said.

"Must be."

She stepped over to the aquarium and watched the fish swim toward the surface: the small angel fish, the swordtails, the Belgian flags with their red eyes, the black widows with their funereal livery. The male ruby barbs wore their magnificent breeding colours: a red glow on the head and foreparts.

John went upstairs to run her bath and she was left alone, weeping silently in front of her son's photo. When Sappho came rubbing against her legs, Lydia bent down and gathered the cat into her arms. Then the phone rang and she heard John answer in the bedroom. She wiped her face on her sleeve.

"It's okay, relax," he shouted down from the landing. "I told her you were in bed."

He returned downstairs and set about putting the dishes away in the dishwasher. Lydia stood on the threshold, the cat in her arms.

"Was it my mother?"

"Yes," John said absently. He then stopped and looked at her closely. "Lydia?"

"I should call her back," she said, speaking to herself.

He put his arm around her waist. "It's all right. You can call her tomorrow."

Lydia looked at her watch. "Yes, okay. I guess I will. It's getting late anyway."

She remained standing, her hand tucked into her robe, as if in search of warmth. Suddenly, a soft, groaning sound escaped her throat and she flung herself against her husband, her face buried in his chest, her arms around his waist.

John closed his eyes. He kissed the top of Lydia's head and stood stroking her back with slow, steady motions.

There was a long silence. From the upstairs bathroom wafted a delicate, familiar fragrance. John placed a coaxing hand against Lydia's back.

"Come, have your bath," he said, steering her toward the staircase. "There'll be plenty of time for everything tomorrow."

"Tomorrow," she muttered, like a sleepy child trying to make sense of a new word, or just delay having to go to bed. But a hot bath was probably what she needed. A hot bath and a good night's sleep.

She followed her husband up the carpeted stairs. They had all but reached the second-floor landing when she noticed a tiny rip on the back of John's pants. It did not, she thought, make sense for a tiny rip on your husband's pants to start you weeping all over again. But this was what happened.

And so she stepped into the bathroom with tears freely splashing out of her eyes. She did not try to explain, but neither did she make any attempt to conceal her grief.

"There, there," John said, his hand at her back. "Give it time, my darling. Just…try to be patient. I love you, you know," he added.

Lydia swiped at her eyes, speaking through her tears. "I love you too," she finally said.

FRIDAY
September 13, 1991

33

It was Friday afternoon, five days after her discharge from St. Margaret's Hospital. The forecast called for showers before the day was over, but for now, the sky showed no sign of impending rain. It was a brilliantly sunny day, with hardly a hint of autumn in the chrysanthemum-scented air.

Lydia set about cleaning the two upper bathrooms. Every day presented the same challenge; every morning she got out of bed determined to keep busy, doing her best to slam the door on thoughts of her recent ordeal. When this proved impossible, she took out her journal and let her grief spill onto its pages.

Sometime after lunch, glancing out the solarium window, she spotted Mrs. Farquhar's daughter-in-law standing on the front lawn in the warm sunshine, cuddling her youngest child. The mother was in her mid-forties and the baby had been a delightful surprise to the parents. Lydia had learned all this from Mrs. Farquhar, but this was the first time she had caught a glimpse of the daughter-in-law, who lived in a West Coast commune with her husband and three children.

The baby was about nine months old and the sight of her bare, plump legs and tiny pink feet had filled Lydia with a devouring tenderness. The mother put the child down in a stroller, then went to pay a dry cleaner's delivery man who had just arrived, bearing winter coats.

Lydia drew away from the window and sat down on one of the loveseats, idly watching a daddy-long-legs crawl up the exposed brick wall. But then her eyes landed on her dead son's photo and she felt clobbered anew, torn between a wild desire to flee to the ends of the earth and an equally intense need to be back in bed, with her husband's arms around her. She shifted her gaze to the urn containing her son's ashes and began quietly weeping, her defeated breasts rising and falling with a quiet breathing.

When, at length, she stood up again, she noticed with some surprise that the Farquhars' baby was now alone on the sunbathed lawn, sleeping peacefully in her stroller, clutching a small rubber giraffe by its long orange neck. She supposed that the mother had left the baby on the front lawn because her teenage boys were playing ball in the back; possibly, too, because that part of the garden did not get much afternoon sun.

For a few minutes, Lydia lingered at the window and watched the baby sleep with her face resting sideways. The baby girl was wearing a white bonnet, but some of her hair had escaped the frilly border, one tendril peeping over her forehead, another prettily decorating her flushed cheek. She looked enchanting, dozing there in the fall sunshine, but it was the possessive intensity with which she clutched the giraffe in her sleep that mysteriously tugged at Lydia's heart.

Although the houses in that part of Outremont were set high up, well above busy Côte-Sainte-Catherine, she was beginning to feel vaguely anxious on behalf of her neighbour's family. John had occasionally accused her of letting her imagination run wild but, after all, if news reports were to be believed, it was apparently not all that difficult to snatch a baby and walk away with it. What if a passing stranger—some unbalanced woman who desperately wanted a child—took it into her head to run off with the Farquhars' adorable baby? She could be someone's mad relative, or a cleaning lady, or just a random driver delivering a parcel or takeout.

It was unlikely, Lydia told herself sternly—extremely unlikely—but no, not impossible. A lonely, deeply disturbed woman might tell herself that any mother who would leave a baby unattended outdoors had to be an unfit parent; and that, in any case, this negligent mother already had two healthy sons.

Lydia was certain that, even on her most despairing day, she herself could never succumb to such an insane impulse, but it proved impossible to suppress her own recent experience at St. Margaret's. With an inner shudder, she recalled the moment when she herself had been tempted to pick up a fretting newborn. She probably would have, too, had a nurse not chanced to come by. Would she have gone so far as to offer her breast to the hungry child?

Maybe. Probably.

Flustered by her own thoughts, Lydia tried to anchor herself in domestic tasks. She began to collect summer clothes to be washed, but seemed unable to arrest the fictional scenario unfolding in her restless mind. Would the kidnapper look like a woman no one would dream of suspecting, or was she more likely to have a disheveled and frantic air?

Impossible to say, but not at all hard to imagine a childless stranger leaning into a crying baby's crib, making soothing noises, only to find herself overcome by unbearable longing. The woman might never have planned to kidnap a baby, yet Lydia could vividly see her snatching the unsupervised infant and fleeing with it, heedless of fear and scruples. How would such a tragic episode end? Lydia could not decide. The fictional possibilities seemed as intriguing as the potential twists of life itself.

She was loading the washing machine when she remembered the creative writing course John had talked her into taking last winter. She regretted her decision to withdraw from the course, but maybe she could register for another? It was only early September; it might still be possible to gain admission to the fall session.

Lydia made a mental note to phone the university on Monday morning, hoping she would not end up changing her mind. She knew that John had been thinking only of children's books when he urged her to take the course, but no matter: he would be relieved to find her finally interested in something.

More than just interested, as it turned out. Lydia surprised herself by feeling something akin to eagerness. She feared it might not last, but allowed herself, for now, to savour the warm sensation spreading in the vicinity of her heart. What if her husband had been right on that long-ago winter night? What if she really had missed her calling?

34

At day's end, the Gabriels' solarium, with its tropical plants and illuminated aquarium, had an air of remote, isolated tranquility, like a private, leafy island harbouring a privileged mystery. It had been a beautiful, shimmering afternoon, but now it was almost evening and the weather was starting to change.

Having prepared a stir-fry dinner, Lydia lit a lamp, thinking to review her recent journal entries while waiting for her husband to come home from the office. She paused at the window, watching Mrs. Farquhar's grandsons romp outdoors. It was growing dark, but the twins seemed blessed with boundless energy, chasing each other back and forth on the fading lawn. John was running late today, though it seemed later than it actually was because the days had been steadily shrinking.

Try to get involved with something when you get out of here.

Tired from her afternoon exertions, Lydia opened a bottle of Chardonnay and sat mulling over

Dr. Seager's words, then her own idea of starting a local branch for bereaved mothers. She was sure that her friend Marika, who was a social worker, might be in a position to help; there were bound to be others.

She thought, sadly, of Dr. Seager, whom she might never see again, and then of John surprising her yesterday by raising the previously rejected idea of adopting a child. They had recently heard that China was about to open its doors to foreign adoption. Her husband, she knew, was worried about her, all alone with her thoughts, day after day. She understood he was trying to help, but all she was able to say yesterday was that, yes, she would think about it. Maybe someday.

"Of course," John hastened to reassure her. "Meanwhile, think about where you'd like to go this winter. I just wanted to let you know that I'm all for it now. Whatever I might have said in the past."

"Thank you," Lydia said simply.

She was not sure about Bora Bora or the Seychelles, but one thing she knew now without any doubt: she had been wrong to think she could never love another woman's child. She took a sip of wine and was reaching for her journal when a new, unexpectedly stirring, possibility insinuated itself into her thoughts.

She had never considered writing about her own loss, except in these private pages meant only for her own eyes. But what if she could write a story, or even a novel, about her own recent ordeal? Did she have what it took to do this? Would a creative writing course help her get there?

"Just think," she recalled John saying all those months ago. "You may someday walk into a library and find a book with your own name on it. Wouldn't that be exciting?"

Exciting? The idea of writing her own novel seemed thrilling and terrifying in equal measure. Lydia topped up her wine glass and sat for a while, absorbed in thought, reflecting on a quotation she'd come across in a new biography she had recently finished reading.

"Human language is like a cracked kettle on which we beat out tunes to make bears dance, while all the time longing to move the stars to pity."

The words were Gustave Flaubert's, but, right then and there, Lydia decided that if she ever managed to write a novel about her personal experience, a fictional plot could perhaps incorporate a bereaved stranger running off with another woman's baby. Would that make for a more compelling story? Would anyone want to read it?

Oh, God, was she drunk already, allowing herself to get carried away like this? Her husband had observed, years ago, her tendency to make impetuous decisions in moments of acute distress. Was this an impetuous idea?

Lydia put down her half-empty wine glass. She headed back to the kitchen, listening for the crunch of wheels in the driveway. It was time to put the rice on and direct her thoughts in more practical directions. Outside, the sky was quickly darkening; an owl began to call, lodged in the swaying poplar.

Helen had brought back a colourful Mexican cardigan. Lydia picked it up and wrapped it around her shoulders. It was beginning to rain, but one of the windows was slightly ajar and, through it, Lydia could hear Mrs. Farquhar call her roaming cat to come back in. The little baby girl would by now be safely indoors, in the bosom of her family. John was on his way home. Helen was coming for lunch tomorrow. On Sunday, it would finally be time to go visit her grieving mother.

A deep sigh escaped Lydia's throat. She reached for the rice jar, talking to her cats. Sappho and Arion had slipped into the kitchen and were now huddled at her feet, as if to keep her toes warm. The owl went on calling. Every now and then, there was the hiss of an autumnal breeze sweeping through grass and hedges. Lydia glanced at the kitchen clock. It was going on seven. She began to empty the dishwasher, while Mrs. Farquhar went on calling, calling.

It was something the old woman did daily around dinnertime, as predictable as the evening news. She called a few times, holding the screen door open, repeating the cat's name in her high, tremulous voice.

Setting the table, Lydia found unexpected comfort in her elderly neighbour's familiar voice, the muffled singing of crickets below her open window, the whisper of falling rain. Eventually, the elderly widow stopped calling and the evening all at once was stunningly quiet, except for the intermittent cry of the hidden owl and, somewhere in the glittering distance, the steady rumble of cars heading home under the weeping stars.

Acknowledgements

Excerpts from the novel originally appeared in the *Ottawa Citizen Magazine* and in *WordCity Lit*.

I am grateful to the Canada Council for its generous financial support, to Jane Troop and Brabna Gillett for invaluable information about maternity wards, to Woodeline Dorlean for more nursing feedback, to Drs. Sam Shuldiner and David Hemmings for medical information, and to Kim Echlin, William Kotzwinkle, and Don Winkler for their interest and support. Thanks, too, to Olga Stein and Darcie Friesen Hossack for their early feedback, and to Leila Marshy, Baraka Books' editor, for helping me improve this challenging story.

Last but not least, I am deeply indebted to the following books.

Swimmer in the Secret Sea by William Kotzwinkle (Chronicle Books, 1994).

When Pregnancy Fails: Families Coping with Miscarriage, Stillbirth, and Infant Death by Susan Borg and Judith Lasker (Beacon Press, 1981).

Song for Sarah: A Mother's Journey Through Grief and Beyond, by Paula D'Arcy (Harold Shaw Publishers, 1979).

The Bereaved Parent by Harriet Sarnoff Schiff (Penguin Books, 1977).

Also from Baraka Books or QC Fiction

FICTON

My Thievery of the People by Leila Marshy
Saints Rest by Luke Francis Beirne
Looking for Her by Carolyn Marie Souaid
The Thickness of Ice by Gerard Beirne
Dear Haider by Lili Zeng
In the Shadow of Crows by M.V. Feehan
Morel by Maxime Raymond Bock (translated by Mélissa Bull) (QC FICTION)

NON-FICTON

Eyes Have Seen, From Mississippi to Montreal by Fred Anderson
Einstein on Israel and Zionism, New Enriched Edition by Fred Jerome
Arsenic mon amour by Jean-Lou David and Gabrielle Izaguirré-Falardeau

Printed by Imprimerie Gauvin
Gatineau, Québec